"How am I going ___ ___ of Shelby when she hates me?" Hannah murmured.

Daniel smiled. "She doesn't hate you. She's scared, and she's known me longer."

"Two minutes longer because you're the one who found her on my doorstep!" Hannah said. "That doesn't make sense."

"Just as it doesn't make sense she doesn't like you. Who knows what goes on in the heads of *bopplin*?" He shampooed little Shelby's hair, taking care not to get suds in her eyes. "I'll make you a deal, Hannah." He began to rinse Shelby's fine hair. "You help me by moving the bees at the bridge, and I'll help you learn how to take care of Shelby. In addition, I'll do all I can to find your *daed*."

Hannah nodded, but didn't speak.

Knowing he shouldn't push her further, he lifted the *kind* out and wrapped her in a towel before her wiggling sent water all over the bathroom. He watched Hannah's face, knowing she wished he'd walked away as he had before.

But she needed his help. And he needed hers.

Jo Ann Brown has always loved stories with happy-ever-after endings. A former military officer, she is thrilled to have the chance to write stories about people falling in love. She is also a photographer, and she travels with her husband of more than thirty years to places where she can snap pictures. They live in Nevada with three children and a spoiled cat. Drop her a note at joannbrownbooks.com.

Books by Jo Ann Brown

Love Inspired

Amish Hearts

Amish Homecoming
An Amish Match
His Amish Sweetheart
An Amish Reunion

Love Inspired Historical

Matchmaking Babies

Promise of a Family
Family in the Making
Her Longed-For Family

Sanctuary Bay

The Dutiful Daughter
A Hero for Christmas
A Bride for the Baron

An Amish Reunion

Jo Ann Brown

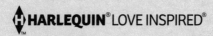

Recycling programs
for this product may
not exist in your area.

LOVE INSPIRED BOOKS

ISBN-13: 978-0-373-89903-6

An Amish Reunion

Copyright © 2016 by Jo Ann Ferguson

This edition published by arrangement with Love Inspired Books.

® and TM are trademarks of Love Inspired Books, used under license.
Trademarks indicated with ® are registered in the United States Patent
and Trademark Office, the Canadian Intellectual Property Office and in
other countries.

www.Harlequin.com

Printed in U.S.A.

Then said He unto me, "Fear not, Daniel:
for from the first day that thou didst set
thine heart to understand, and to chasten thyself
before thy God, thy words were heard,
and I am come for thy words."
—*Daniel* 10:12

For Janet Jones Bann
Thanks for all you do for all of us,
especially being my friend

Chapter One

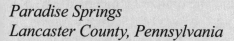

Paradise Springs
Lancaster County, Pennsylvania

The knock came at the worst possible moment.

Hannah Lambright had her *grossmammi* partway to her bed where she could look out, through the cold rain, at the covered bridge over Hunter's Mill Creek until she fell asleep for her afternoon nap. *Grossmammi* Ella depended on Hannah to help her. She refused to use a cane, not wanting to be considered old, though she'd recently celebrated her 90th birthday.

Smoothing the blanket over her *grossmammi*, who'd already closed her eyes, Hannah hurried from the room. She wiped her hands on her black apron and pushed loose strands of hair under her white *kapp*. The impatient rapping continued. She opened the door. Words fled from her mouth and her brain as she stared at a handsome face she'd never expected to see at her door. She couldn't be mistaken about the identity of the man with sleek black hair beneath his dripping straw hat and deep blue eyes set below assertive brows. Her momentary hope that she was looking at his twin brother vanished when she noticed the cleft in his chin.

"Daniel Stoltzfus, why are you here?" she asked.

"Is she yours?"

Only then did she realize Daniel held a wicker container about the size of a laundry basket. A little girl, her golden hair in uneven braids sticking out like a bug's antennae, was curled, half-asleep in the basket. Chocolate crumbs freckled her cheeks. The *kind* wore an *Englisch*-style pink overall and a shirt with puffy sleeves. She couldn't have been more than eighteen months old.

"Mine?" she choked.

The little girl's dark brown eyes opened. Her chubby, adorable face displayed the unmistakable characteristics of Down syndrome.

"I was on my way to the covered bridge when I saw her in your side yard," he replied. "By the time my buggy stopped and I could get out, she'd disappeared behind the house."

"My honeybees are out there! Did she get stung?"

"I don't think so. Is this *kind* yours?"

She recoiled from the strong emotions darkening his blue eyes. Behind his question, she heard unspoken accusations. An answer of *ja* would mean not only was she an unmarried woman with a *kind*, but she let the toddler wander near her beehives.

After the five months she and Daniel had walked out together three years ago, did he know so little about her? Didn't he know she was the dependable one? As she'd been since her *mamm* died when she was ten years old. When she dared to trust someone again, she'd chosen Daniel Stoltzfus, who'd broken her heart.

"I don't know who she is," Hannah said, determined to keep her thoughts to herself. "Just because she was in my yard—"

"And this basket was on your porch. She must have crawled out of it."

"Why would someone leave her on my front porch?"

"I've got no idea." He glanced over his shoulder. "It's raining. Can we come in?"

Hannah could think of a dozen reasons to say no, but nodded. She couldn't leave a young *kind* out in the cold and damp…nor Daniel.

He set the basket on the well-worn sofa and squatted beside it. When the little girl sat and began to whimper, he said, "It's okay, *liebling*. You're safe."

She didn't know if the little girl knew the word meant sweetheart, but the *kind* began to calm as she gazed at him, trying to figure out who he was.

Hannah bit back a sad laugh. After months with him, she'd been shocked when he turned out not to be the man she'd thought he was. She shook those thoughts aside. The *kind* should be her sole concern.

The little girl moved, and Hannah heard a crackle. A crumpled and wet envelope was stuck in the basket. Hannah took it and removed a single piece of wet paper. How long had the basket and the toddler been in the rain? She peeled the damp edges apart and was relieved the writing hadn't been smudged.

"What does it say?" Daniel asked.

She read aloud, "Shelby is your sister. Take care of her." Looking at the *kind*, she asked, "Are you Shelby?"

The little girl blinked.

"I guess Shelby *is* her name." He began to make faces at the little girl. "Does it say anything else?"

Hannah gasped when she saw the signature. *Daed.*

In the fifteen years since he'd left after her *mamm*'s death, her *daed* hadn't written her a single letter. At first, she'd thought it was because he'd been placed under the *bann* when he abandoned his faith along with his only *kind*. Later, he'd sent postcards from the places around the United States and Canada. Nevada and Florida. California and Mississippi. Manitoba and Texas. Never anywhere near Paradise Springs. And never with any message other than *Daed*.

Until now.

What was going on?

"Is it signed?" Daniel asked.

She nodded, unable to speak. Had her *daed* been right outside the door? Why hadn't he knocked? Did he think she'd turn him away? She sighed as she realized he might have been afraid she wouldn't take the basket from him. The rules of the *bann* were clear—she could speak with him, though her words should be focused on persuading him to confess his sins and return to their plain life. She couldn't eat at the same table or take a piece of paper from his hand. The whole community hoped a shunning would convince an offender to repent; then family and friends would welcome him into the fold as if the *bann* had never happened. As God forgave, so should those who loved Him.

"Who signed it, Hannah?" Daniel's voice was as gentle as when he'd spoken to the little girl.

She gulped, trying to swallow past the lump in her throat. How could *Daed* have left without seeing her again? Feeling as hurt as the day she'd discovered he'd jumped the fence into the *Englisch* world, she whispered, "My *daed*."

Daniel's eyes widened. He was as stunned as she was. More than once, while they'd been courting, she'd talked about her hope to see her *daed* again.

Under a stained blanket, she saw a lump. She lifted out two plastic bags. The handles were tied together. She hooked her finger in the top of one and pulled. The bag tore, and tiny clothing, most in shades of pink, scattered across the floor.

"Her clothes, I'd guess," Daniel said as he picked up the little girl. He bounced the *kind* and tried to keep her from pulling off his straw hat at the same time.

The sight was so endearing Hannah smiled in spite of herself. When a chuckle escaped, he looked at her in astonishment.

"Are you okay?" he asked.

"I don't know." That was the most honest answer she had. One minute, she'd been going about her daily routine. The next, the man she'd once believed wanted to marry her was standing on her porch with a *boppli* in a basket. "I don't know what to do or say."

"You could start by holding your sister."

Sister! She'd never had a sister…or a brother. Her extended family lived in northern New York,

too far away except for an occasional visit when
one of her cousins married. It'd been her and
Grossmammi Ella since her *daed* left. She'd
dreamed of having a sibling. As a *kind*, she'd
prayed night after night for one. Had God answered her prayer like this?

She held out her arms, and Daniel shifted the
kind so Hannah could take her.

With a cry, Shelby clung to him. She buried
her face in his shoulder, rubbing chocolate into
his coat, and wrapped her tiny arms around his
neck. Her sobs trembled along her.

"Give her a minute," Daniel said before murmuring in *Englisch*, "Shelby, look at Hannah.
She likes little girls."

She shrieked as if caught in a swarm of bees.

Hannah yanked her hands away. Her little sister, the blessed gift she'd yearned for, wanted
nothing to do with her. And Shelby cuddled
against the man who'd wanted nothing to do
with her either.

Daniel watched the flurry of emotions sweep
across Hannah's face. Frustration. Uncertainty.
Regret. Pain. He'd seen the last when she'd found
him flirting with other girls. The memory of
that evening had lurked in his thoughts for three
years, a constant reminder that if he let someone else come as close to his heart as she had,

he could wound that person as badly. Better to keep things light and laugh with every girl instead of making a marvelous one like Hannah cry. He wasn't going to take a chance of that happening again. He'd learned his lesson the hardest possible way.

He wouldn't have come to the stone-end farmhouse where she lived with her great-grandmother and her bees if he'd had another choice. But he needed to ask for a favor. A big one, and he wasn't sure if Hannah would agree when they hadn't spoken in three years.

He should look away from her pretty face, but he couldn't. How was it possible that Hannah had become even more beautiful? He hadn't seen her since that evening she'd walked out of his life. His older brother Amos had occasionally mentioned Hannah bringing honey from her hives to sell at his grocery store. Each time, Daniel had changed the subject. He didn't want to think about how he'd ruined everything between him and Hannah.

In the rainy day's dim light, her hair was the shade of her honey. Drawn under a green bandana that matched her dress, her hair framed her oval face. Her chocolate-brown eyes displayed her feelings. She'd never been able to hide her thoughts. Now she was upset because the *kind* refused to go to her.

"It's okay, Shelby," he said in *Englisch* because he suspected she didn't understand *Deitsch*, the language the Amish spoke. "You don't have to go anywhere you don't want to."

The *kind* tilted her head; then she gave him a big grin, showing off tiny teeth. Her eyes crinkled closed, and he saw the striking resemblance between the little girl and Hannah. The shape of their faces, those dark eyes and the shiny, honey-gold hair were almost identical.

"Is your great-grandmother here?" he asked.

"She's taking a nap." Hannah continued to stare at Shelby with distress.

"With all this noise?"

"*Grossmammi* Ella takes a nap every day from one until two-thirty. Even if she's awake, she won't come out until two-thirty." Her lips quirked. "No matter what."

"That's weird."

"It's her way."

His nose wrinkled. "Someone could use a diaper change." He ran a finger along the *kind*'s tiny arm. "And she's cold. What she needs is a *gut*, warm bath."

"She won't let me give her one." Again the dismay filled her voice.

"I'll help." He hesitated, then said, "If you'll let me."

She glanced toward the front door. As clearly

as if she'd shouted, he knew she wanted him to leave.

"This isn't about what happened to us, Hannah. It's about what's happened to your little sister."

Her face blanched, but she squared her shoulders. He recognized the motion. Whenever Hannah set her shoulders, she was ready to take on a disagreeable task. He'd prefer not to think she saw him as that.

"The bathroom is this way." She gathered the scattered clothes and bags before leading him into the simple kitchen. She opened the door next to the woodstove and motioned for him to enter.

He couldn't ignore how Shelby tightened her arms around him when he passed Hannah. He wanted to tell the *kind* she was making a big mistake. Hannah would do anything for anyone. Everybody knew they could depend on her.

He, on the other hand... He frowned. Trying to explain to Hannah why he'd done what he did would be a waste of breath. He'd failed her three years ago, and he doubted he'd do better now. He couldn't find the words to tell her how important it was for him to own a business as his older brothers did. He couldn't admit how scared and worried he'd been to try to handle the challenges of that along with a wife and family. He'd wanted to be honest, but how could he tell the most dependable person he knew he wasn't sure she could depend on him? And then he'd proved that by flirting with someone else. He couldn't remember which girl it'd been.

Pushing aside self-recriminations, he carried Shelby into the bathroom as Hannah put the clothes on a counter by the sink. It was a small room. The big bathtub must have been installed for Hannah's *grossmammi*. The tub had a door in the side and held a chair where someone could sit while bathing. Hannah made sure the door was locked and lifted out the chair. She shoved it as far toward the window as she could. After turning on the faucet and testing the water to make sure it was neither too hot nor too cold, she faced him.

"Will she let me take her?" she asked.

"Let me get her started, and we'll see how she does. Can you get a towel and washcloth while I put her into the tub?"

"*Ja*. They're right behind you. I'll get—"

He put out an arm to halt her from reaching past him. When her hand touched his arm, she flinched as if he were connected to an electric circuit and she'd gotten zapped.

Pulling down a towel, she shoved it into his hand. "Why are you here?"

He set the little girl on the floor and knelt to unhook the straps on her overalls. That gave him an excuse not to look at Hannah while he asked for her help. Shelby wiggled as he drew off her wet clothes. Once she was undressed and her braids undone, he rinsed off her bottom before placing her in the tub. She slapped the water and giggled when it flew everywhere, including the front of his shirt.

Taking a washcloth and soap from Hannah, he began washing the *kind*'s face and arms. He kept one hand on Shelby's shoulder as he said, "I've been hired to strengthen the Hunter's Mill Creek Bridge so it can be used for heavier traffic again, and I need your help."

"I'm not much *gut* with a hammer."

Was she jesting? He didn't dare take his eyes off the little girl to see. Deciding it'd be better not to respond to her comment, he said, "I can't begin work until something is done about the beehive in a rotting board beneath the bridge."

"Bees? What kind?" Excitement sifted into her voice.

"I think they're honeybees."

"You're not sure?"

He risked a quick glance at Hannah who sat on the chair she'd taken from the tub. She watched how he cleaned the toddler. "You're the expert. Not me. I can't tell one kind of bee from another. They need to be moved so nobody gets stung while we're working on the bridge. I considered spraying them, but I've heard there aren't as many honeybees as there used to be."

"*Ja*, that's true. Pesticides and pests have killed them."

"That's why I decided to check with an expert—with *you*—before I contacted an exterminator." He cupped his hand and poured warm water over Shelby's head, wetting it so he could wash her hair. He kept his other hand above her eyes to prevent water from flowing into them.

"*Danki* for checking, Daniel. Many people don't. They spray the hive, never stopping to think we need honeybees to pollinate our crops." She held out a bottle of shampoo. "You're *gut* with her."

"Practice. My sister Esther was a lot younger than the rest of us, and I used to help *Mamm*. And I've got a bunch of nieces and nephews." He edged back. "Do you want to put the shampoo on her hair?"

"Do you think she'll let me?"

"One way to know." Keeping his right hand on Shelby's arm, he stepped aside.

Hannah eased past him, making sure not an inch of her brushed against him, not even the hem of her apron or *kapp* strings. She bent over the tub and smiled. "Let's get your pretty hair clean, Shelby."

The *kind*'s lower lip trembled, and thick tears rolled down her cheeks.

Her face falling, Hannah edged away. She wrapped her arms around herself as Shelby returned to her playing when Daniel stood by the tub again.

"How am I going to take care of her when she hates me?" Hannah murmured.

"She doesn't hate you. She's scared, and she's known me longer."

"Two minutes! That doesn't make sense."

"Just as it doesn't make sense she doesn't like you. Who knows what goes on in the heads of *bopplin*?" He shampooed Shelby's hair, taking care not to get suds in her eyes. He'd stop at his brother's grocery store and get some shampoo made for *boppli* before he returned to work on the bridge tomorrow.

At that thought, he said, "I'll make you a deal, Hannah." He began to rinse Shelby's fine hair. "You help me by moving the bees, and I'll help you learn how to take care of Shelby. In addition, I'll do all I can to find your *daed*."

"How will you find *Daed*?"

"I can ask the police—"

She shook her head. "It's not our way to involve *Englischers* in our business."

"It may need to be if you want to know the truth about your *daed*."

"I don't know." She dragged the reluctant words out.

"If the bishop says it's okay, will you?" He hated backing her into a corner, but she must see that they needed help in the extraordinary situation.

Hannah nodded, but didn't speak.

Knowing he shouldn't push her further, he lifted the *kind* out and wrapped her in a towel before her wiggling sent water all over the bathroom. He watched Hannah's face, knowing she wished he'd walked away as he had before. But she needed his help. And he needed hers. None of the men he'd hired would get close to the bridge supports while the bees were there.

Putting Shelby on the floor, he grabbed for the unopened bag. He couldn't reach it.

"What do you need?" Hannah asked.

Your agreement to move the bees, he wanted to say, but didn't. She was upset, and he didn't want to make her feel worse. "A diaper."

She opened the bag and frowned. "Um…"

"Let me look." He took the bag, and with a smile, he pulled out a disposable diaper. He diapered the toddler and pulled a warm shirt and trousers from the counter to dress her.

Hannah handed him a pair of socks. "I'm sorry. I've only seen cloth diapers before."

"It's okay." He hesitated, then said, "If you

want, I can take her to our house. My *mamm* will watch her."

"No!"

"Are you sure?"

"*Ja.* My *daed* could come back. She needs to be here when he does."

Daniel didn't argue, though he had his doubts any man who abandoned two daughters would return. "Did you see how I put the diaper on her?"

"*Ja.* It's easy."

"It is. As you're going to need my help with her, what do you say? Do we have a deal? I'll help you with Shelby as well as try to find your *daed*, and you'll move the bees for me. Do we have a deal?"

"All right, Daniel," she said as if agreeing to a truce with her worst enemy. He flinched, hoping she didn't consider him that. He knew he'd have time to find out when she went on, "It's a deal."

Chapter Two

As soon as the words agreeing to the plan with Daniel left her lips, Hannah wanted to take them back. But how could she turn aside his help? Looking at the little girl perched on Daniel's knee while he sat on the edge of the tub, Hannah knew she needed his assistance. Her great-grandmother might want to help, but the elderly woman was fragile. *Grossmammi* Ella couldn't chase an active toddler. Though nothing had ever been said, Hannah often wondered if her *grossmammi* resented having a ten-year-old dumped on her to raise.

"Gut," Daniel said as he shifted Shelby into his arms as he stood.

He avoided Hannah's eyes, and she couldn't meet his either. Suddenly the bathroom seemed as small as a phone shack.

It seemed to shrink farther when he went on,

"I'm glad you're willing to be sensible about this, Hannah. After all, what happened in the past is best left there."

"I agree." That wasn't exactly the truth, but she wanted to put an end to this strained conversation. She couldn't imagine how their "deal" would work. Daniel might be able to leave the past in the past, but she wasn't sure she could. A heated aura of humiliation surrounded her whenever she thought of how he'd dumped her without an explanation.

Shelby chirped and tugged at his hair, interrupting Hannah's bleak thoughts. A *kind* depended on her. For that reason—and to protect a hive of what she hoped were healthy honeybees—she would work with Daniel. She wouldn't trust him. She'd learned her lesson.

Hearing a soft chime from the timer on the kitchen stove, Hannah gathered the wet towel and washcloth. She tossed them in the tub and ignored Daniel's surprise when she left them there.

"Do you have something in the oven?" he asked.

"No. My great-grandmother sets the timer every afternoon before going to rest in her room. About fifteen minutes after it chimes, she'll come out. I try to have a cup of tea ready for her.

"I should get going then."

"But the bees—"

He pointed toward the window where water

ran down the glass. "Let's put that off until the rain stops. We can go tomorrow morning."

"That makes sense." At least one thing had today. Everything else, from Daniel's appearance at her door to the idea her *daed* might have been there moments before, had been bizarre and painful. Why hadn't *Daed* knocked on the door?

A fresh wave of grief struck her as hard as the rain battered the window. Had *Daed* thought she wouldn't want to see him? Or did he think *Grossmammi* Ella would refuse to let him in? Hannah would have talked with him on the porch. She wouldn't have been able to hug him while he was under the *bann*, but she would have welcomed him home and asked him why he'd left her behind. Why hadn't he come home? And, when he did, why did he leave Shelby without letting Hannah know he was there?

"If you need anything before I come back," Daniel said, "let me know."

She frowned. "How? I can't leave a toddler and my great-grandmother here alone."

"My brother has a phone in the barn. I'll give you the number."

"Danki." She regretted snapping at him. She couldn't let dismay with her *daed* color her conversations with others. Maybe Daniel was right. Leaving the past in the past was a *gut* idea. "Our *Englisch* neighbors let me use their phone when

it's necessary. We should be okay. There are plenty of diapers and clothing in the bag for tonight."

"Gut." He left the bathroom.

Suddenly there seemed to be enough oxygen to take a breath, and Hannah sucked in a quick one. She needed to get herself on an even keel if Daniel was visiting for the next few days. How long would it take to learn how to take care of Shelby? Not that long, she was sure.

Her certainty wavered when Daniel paused in the living room and held out Shelby to her. Smiling and cooing at the *kind*, Hannah took her.

The room erupted into chaos when the toddler shrieked at the top of her lungs and reached out toward him, her body stiff with the indignity of being handed off to Hannah.

"Go!" Hannah ordered.

"Are you sure?" Daniel asked.

"Ja." Stretching out his leaving would just upset everyone more.

Shelby's crying became heartbreaking as Daniel slipped out and closed the door behind him. She squirmed so hard, Hannah put her down.

Teetering as if the floor rocked beneath her, Shelby rushed to the door. She stretched her hand toward the knob, but couldn't reach it. Leaning her face against the door, she sobbed.

Hannah was tempted to join her in tears. The

sight of the distraught *kind* shattered her heart.
When she took a step forward, wanting to comfort Shelby, the toddler's crying rose in pitch like
a fire siren. Hannah jumped back, unsure what
to do. She silenced the longing to call after Daniel and ask him to calm the *kind*. As soon as he
left once more, Shelby might react like this all
over again.

Hating to leave the little girl by the door, Hannah edged toward the kitchen. She kept her eyes
on Shelby while setting the kettle on the stove to
heat. The *kind* didn't move an inch while Hannah
took out the tea and a cup for her great-grandmother. Nor when Hannah set a handful of cookies on a plate and poured a small amount of milk
into a glass.

The first thing to put on her list of what she'd
need for the *kind*: plastic cups. Maybe she could
find some with tops so Shelby could drink without spilling. Or was Hannah getting ahead of
herself? She didn't know if the little girl could
drink from a cup.

The door to the downstairs bedroom opened.
Her great-grandmother, Ella Lambright, leaned
one hand on the door frame. She'd left her cane in
the bedroom. Her steps were as unsteady as Shelby's. Unlike the *kind*, her face was lined from
many summers of working in her garden. She
wore a black dress, stockings and shoes as she

had every day since her husband died two years before Hannah's parents had wed.

Hannah rushed to assist her great-grandmother to the kitchen table. The old woman took a single step, then paused as another wail came from beside the front door.

"Who is that?" *Grossmammi* Ella said in her wispy voice. The strings on her *kapp* struck Hannah's cheek as she turned her head to look at the sobbing toddler. The elderly woman's white hair was as thin and crisp as the organdy of her *kapp*. She actually was Hannah's *daed*'s *grossmammi*.

"Her name is Shelby."

"That isn't a plain name." Her snowy brows dropped into a scowl. "And she isn't wearing plain clothes. What is an *Englisch kind* doing here?"

"Sit, and I'll explain."

"Who was that I saw driving away? What did he want here?"

"One thing at a time." Hannah had grown accustomed to *Grossmammi* Ella's impatience. In many ways, her great-grandmother's mind had regressed to the level of a toddler's. Impatient, jumping from one subject to another and with no apparent connection of one thought to the next, focused on her own needs. "That's what a wise woman told me."

"Foolish woman, if you ask me," *Grossmammi* Ella muttered.

Hannah assisted her great-grandmother to sit. Now wasn't the time to mention the wise woman had been *Grossmammi* Ella. Saying that might start an argument because the old woman could be quarrelsome when she felt frustrated, which was often lately.

Hoping she wouldn't make matters worse, Hannah went to Shelby. She knelt, but didn't reach out to the toddler. "Shelby?" she whispered.

The little girl turned toward her, her earth-brown eyes like Hannah's. Heated trails of tears curved along her full cheeks, and her nose was as red as the skin around her eyes. Averting her face, the *kind* began to suck her thumb while she clung to the door.

Hannah waited, not saying anything. When Shelby's eyes grew heavy, the toddler slid to sit and lean her face against the door. The poor little girl was exhausted. Hannah wondered when the *kind* had last slept.

When Shelby's breathing grew slow, Hannah slipped her arms around the toddler. Shelby stiffened, but didn't waken as Hannah placed her on the sofa. Getting a small quilt, Hannah draped it over the little girl.

Straightening, Hannah went to sit beside her great-grandmother. Patting *Grossmammi* Ella's fragile arm, she began to explain what had happened while the old woman was resting. The story sounded unbelievable, but its proof slept on the sofa.

When her great-grandmother asked what Hannah intended to do now, Hannah said, "I don't know."

And she didn't. She hoped God would send her ideas of how to deal with the arrival of an unknown sister, because she had none.

Reuben Lapp's place wasn't on Daniel's way home to the farm where he'd lived his whole life, but he turned his buggy left where he usually turned right and followed the road toward where the sun was setting through the bank of clouds clinging to the hills. It was growing chilly, a reminder winter hadn't left. At least, the rain hadn't turned to sleet or snow.

He'd promised Hannah that he'd help her find out where her *daed* was. Hannah had been willing—albeit reluctantly—for him to speak with Reuben and get the bishop's advice.

Why didn't she want to use every method possible to find her *daed*? Daniel was sure she was as curious as he was about why Shelby had been left on the porch. Yet, she'd hesitated when he mentioned locating her *daed*.

Why?

You could have asked her. His conscience refused to let him ignore the obvious, but he had to admit that Hannah had her hands full when he left. As he closed the Lambrights' door, he'd heard Shelby begin to cry in earnest. He'd almost gone back in, stopping himself because he wanted to get the search for her *daed* started as soon as possible.

Propane lamps were lit in the bishop's large white house when Daniel arrived. He drove past the house and toward the whitewashed barns beyond it. Odors of overturned earth came from the fields. Reuben must be readying them for planting, using what time he had between storms.

Stopping the buggy, Daniel jumped out and walked to the biggest barn where the animals were stabled on the floor above the milking parlor. Through the uneven floorboards, he could hear the cows mooing. The bishop's buggy team nickered as he walked past. Several mules looked over the stall doors, their brown eyes curious if he'd brought treats. He patted each one's neck, knowing they'd had a long day in the fields spreading fertilizer.

He didn't slow as he went down the well-worn steps to the lower floor. The cows stood in stanchions, and the rhythm of the milking machine run by a diesel generator in the small, attached lean-to matched his footsteps.

Reuben, a tall man who was muscular despite his years, stood up from between a pair of black-and-white cows. He held a milk can in each hand. The bishop's thick gray beard was woven with a piece of hay, but Daniel didn't mention it as he greeted the older man.

"You're here late," Reuben said in his deep voice.

"I'd like to get your advice."

The bishop nodded. "I need to put this milk in the dairy tank." He motioned for Daniel to follow him through a doorway.

"Let me take one."

"*Danki*, but they're balanced like this." He hefted the milk cans with the strength of a man half his age.

Reuben had been chosen by the lot to be their bishop before Daniel was born. His districts were fortunate to have his gentle, but stern wisdom as well as his dedication to his responsibilities as their bishop. It wasn't an easy life for a man with a family to support, because those selected by the lot to serve weren't paid.

When Reuben went to the stainless steel tank where the milk was kept cold by the diesel engine, Daniel opened the top and checked that the filter was in place. He stepped back so Reuben could pour the milk in. As soon as both cans were empty, Reuben lifted out the filter and closed the top. He set the filter in a deep soapstone sink to clean later.

Wiping his hands on a ragged towel, Reuben said, "I hear you've got a new job. Fixing the Hunter's Mill Creek Bridge."

"Word gets around fast." He chuckled.

"The Amish grapevine is efficient."

Daniel had to smile. For people who didn't use telephones and computers at home, news still managed to spread through the district. He wondered how long it would take for his neighbors to learn about Shelby. News of a *kind* being left on the Lambrights' front porch was sure to be repeated with the speed of lightning.

"I went out to the bridge today," Daniel said. "No work can be done until some bees are removed."

"Bees?" The bishop leaned against the stainless steel tank. "Doesn't Hannah Lambright keep bees? The bridge is close to her house, ain't so? Maybe she'll be willing to help."

"I've already spoken with her. She'll take care of the bees if I help her with a few things."

"Sounds like an excellent solution." Reuben folded his arms over the ends of his gray beard. He shifted and plucked out the piece of hay. Tossing it aside, he went on, "But from your face, Daniel, and the fact you want to talk with me, I'd guess there's more to the story."

"A lot." In terse detail, Daniel outlined how he'd found the *kind* after she escaped from the basket. He told the bishop about the note from Hannah's *daed*. "Hannah will take care of Shelby, of course, until her *daed* can be found."

"Hannah already carries a heavy load of responsibilities with her great-grandmother. Some days, the old woman seems to lose her way, and Hannah must keep a very close watch on her."

"I offered to help with Shelby."

The bishop nodded. "A *gut* neighbor helps when the load becomes onerous."

"And I also told Hannah I'd come to ask you about whether we should contact the police to get help in finding her *daed*. If you're all right with her talking to the police, she agreed that she will."

Reuben didn't say anything for several minutes, and Daniel knew the bishop was pondering the problem and its ramifications. It was too big and important a decision to make without considering everything that could happen as a result.

Daniel wished his thoughts could focus on finding Hannah's missing *daed*. Instead, his mind kept returning to the woman herself. Not just her beauty, though he'd been beguiled by it. No, he couldn't keep from thinking how gentle and solicitous she was of the *kind* and her great-grandmother.

Some had whispered years ago Hannah was too self-centered, like her *daed* who hadn't spared a thought for his daughter when he jumped the fence and joined the *Englisch* world. Daniel had never seen signs of Hannah being selfish when they were walking out. In fact, it'd been the opposite, because he found she cared too much about him. He hadn't wanted her to get serious about him.

Getting married then, he'd believed, would have made a jumble of his plans to open a construction business. That spring, he'd hoped to submit the paperwork within a few weeks, and he thought being distracted by pretty Hannah might be a problem. In retrospect, it'd been the worst decision he could have made.

He hadn't wanted to hurt Hannah. He'd thought she'd turn her attention to someone who could love her as she deserved to be loved. But he'd miscalculated. Instead of flirting with other young men, she'd stopped attending gatherings, sending word she needed to take care of her great-grandmother. At the time, he'd considered it an excuse, but now wondered if she'd been honest.

But whether she'd been or not, he knew one thing for sure. He'd hurt her, and he'd never forgiven himself. Nor had he asked for her forgiveness as he should have. Days had passed becoming weeks, then months and years, and his opportunity had passed.

"I thought we'd seen the last of Isaac Lambright," Reuben said quietly as if he were talking to himself.

"That's Hannah's *daed*?"

The bishop nodded. "Isaac was the last one I guessed would go into the *Englisch* world. He was a *gut* man, a devout man who prized his neighbors and his plain life. But when his wife sickened, he changed. He began drinking away his pain. After Saloma died, he refused to attend the funeral and he left within days."

"Without Hannah." He didn't make it a question. "But Isaac has come to Paradise Springs and left another daughter behind."

"So it would seem." The bishop sighed. "I see no choice in the matter. The *Englisch* authorities must be notified. Abandoning a *kind* is not only an abomination, but a crime. Has the *kind* said anything to help?"

"Shelby makes sounds she seems to think are words, because she looks at you as if you should know what she's saying. It's babbling."

He nodded. "That was a foolish question. A *kind* without Down syndrome uses only a few words at her age. An old *grossdawdi* at my age forgets such things." His grin came and went swiftly. "But that doesn't change anything as far as going to the police." Again he paused, weighing his next words. "Waiting until tomorrow to contact them shouldn't be a problem. I'd like to take tonight to pray for God's guidance."

"Hannah may be hesitant about talking to the cops because she doesn't want to get her *daed* into trouble."

Reuben put his hand on Daniel's arm. "We must assume Isaac is already in trouble. I can't imagine any other reason for a *daed* to leave another one of his daughters as he has." He sighed. "We'd hoped when Isaac was put under the *bann* that he'd see the errors of his ways. He told me after Saloma's death he'd never come back, not even for Hannah. Now he's done the same thing with another daughter."

"If Shelby is his daughter and not someone's idea of a cruel prank."

"And that, Daniel, is why I'll be talking with the police tomorrow morning. They'll know be the best way to find out what's true and what isn't."

"What will happen if Shelby isn't Hannah's sister?"

The bishop clasped Daniel's shoulder and looked him in the eye. "Let's not seek. The future is in God's hands, so let's let Him lead us where we need to go."

Daniel nodded, bowing his head when the

bishop asked him to join him in prayer. He wished a small part of his heart didn't rebel at the idea of handing over the problem to God. That part longed to do something *now.* Something he—Daniel himself—could do to make a difference and help Hannah.

After all, he owed her that much.

Didn't he?

Chapter Three

As the sun rose the next morning, Hannah wondered how she was going to survive the coming day...and the ones to follow. During the night, which had stretched interminably, Shelby had been inconsolable. Her cries from the room across the upstairs hall from Hannah's had kept *Grossmammi* Ella awake, too, on the first floor. Hannah had spent the night trying to get them—and herself—back to sleep. She'd managed the latter an hour before dawn.

Then she'd been awoken what seemed seconds later by the sound of her neighbors working in the field between her house and theirs. The Jones family were *Englischers*, which meant Barry Jones used rumbling tractors and other mechanized equipment in his fields. Usually Hannah was up long before he started work, but not after a night of walking the floor with an anguished toddler and calming her great-grand-mother who was outraged at the suggestion her beloved grandson had left another *kind* on her doorstep.

Hannah dressed and brushed her hair into place. She reached for a bandana to cover it, then picked up her *kapp*. Daniel had said he was going to talk to Reuben Lapp before he came back this morning. It was possible the bishop might visit to discuss Shelby's situation. She hoped he would have some sage advice to offer her.

Lots of sage advice…or any sort of advice. She could use every tidbit to raise a toddler who screamed at the sight of her.

"Keeping my eyes open instead of falling asleep on my feet is the smartest thing I can do," she murmured as she slipped down the stairs.

Passing her great-grandmother's bedroom door, she was relieved it was closed. *Gross-mammi* Ella had been soothed about Shelby's arrival because Hannah assured her great-grand-mother the *kind* wouldn't be with them long. She let *Grossmammi* Ella believe that Hannah's *daed* would return straightaway to collect Shelby.

The situation wasn't made easier because the elderly woman's hearing was failing as fast as her memory. The toddler's cries could slice through concrete, so the noise must be extra jarring for

Grossmammi Ella who missed many quieter sounds. No wonder her nerves were on edge.

Hannah whispered an almost silent prayer of gratitude that *Grossmammi* Ella and the *kind* were still asleep. She doubted the peace would last long, and she needed to figure out what she absolutely had to do that day. She guessed most of her day would be focused on her abruptly expanded family. For the first time in a week, it wasn't raining, so Daniel would want her to check the hive.

She sighed. That would be difficult because she couldn't leave either her great-grandmother or the toddler alone. Though the covered bridge was down the road only a couple hundred feet, going would mean taking *Grossmammi* Ella and Shelby with her unless someone was at the house to keep an eye on them. She'd ask Daniel to do that while she went to figure out what she'd need to move the bees.

Maybe Daniel would have answers about her *daed* when he returned. His brother Amos ran the grocery store, and he may have heard something. It was even possible *Daed* had stopped at the store at the Stoltzfus Family Shops. No, that was unlikely. Why would he go where someone might recognize him?

Oh, Daed, why didn't you knock on our door? I would have listened to you, and perhaps Shelby

*wouldn't be distressed with me if she'd seen you
and me together.*

There weren't answers, which is why, during
the night while she walked the floor with Shelby,
trying to get the little girl to go to sleep, Hannah had known Daniel's suggestion to get Reuben's advice about contacting the police was *gut*.
The police had ways of obtaining information no
plain person did. She had to concentrate on what
was best for Shelby.

With a sigh as she put ground *kaffi* into the
pot on the propane stove, she reminded herself,
until she learned how to take care of the toddler
and removed the bees from the covered bridge,
Daniel would be part of her life. That should last
only a few days; then he'd be gone again. *Gut*,
because she didn't want to let herself or her great-
grandmother or Shelby become dependent upon
him. She'd do as she promised Daniel, and then
she'd go on with her life without him.

As she had before.

A cup of fresh *kaffi* did little to wake Hannah.
She was halfway through her second one when
she heard faint cries upstairs. Putting the cup on
the counter, she hurried to the toddler's room.

Shelby was standing in the crib Hannah
had wrestled down from the attic last night.
Grossmammi Ella kept everything, and Hannah
was glad the old crib was still in the house. Shel-

by's diaper was half-off, and big tears washed down her face. The sight of the forlorn *kind* made Hannah want to weep, too. Again she had to fight her exasperation with her *daed*. Being angry wouldn't help her or Shelby.

"Hush, little one," she crooned as she gathered the *kind* into her arms, hoping Shelby would throw her tiny arms around Hannah's neck.

Instead the toddler stiffened and screeched out her fury. Hannah longed to tell her everything would be okay, but she wouldn't lie to her little sister, though she doubted the toddler understood her. So far, it seemed Shelby comprehended simple words and phrases in *Englisch*. Nothing more, and Hannah hadn't been able to decipher her babblings.

Daed probably wouldn't have spoken to her in *Deitsch*, and it was unlikely Shelby's *mamm* knew the language. Or would she? Who *was* Shelby's *mamm*?

In the chaos of yesterday, Hannah hadn't given the toddler's *mamm* much thought. Where was she? Did she know her *kind* had been left alone on the front porch? Most important, Hannah thought as the little girl leaned her face against her shoulder, would Shelby's *mamm* want her back?

All questions she couldn't answer. What she could do was get Shelby cleaned and fed.

Hannah soon had the little girl, despite Shelby's attempts to escape, in a fresh diaper and clothes. Another pair of pink overalls. She wondered if those were all Shelby wore. Her white shirt today had pink and blue turtles on it. Hannah needed to make clothes for the little girl, but the pressing matter was diapers. She had only about a half dozen on the dresser.

She came down the stairs with Shelby and saw *Grossmammi* Ella was awake and in the kitchen waiting for her breakfast. Exactly as she did every morning, but this day was different.

Putting Shelby in the high chair she'd found in the cellar, Hannah handed the toddler some crackers to keep her busy while she scrambled eggs for them. That seemed to quiet the *kind* who focused her attention on breaking crackers into the tiniest possible pieces.

Hannah gave her great-grandmother a kiss on her wizened cheek. "*Gute mariye, Grossmammi* Ella," she said with a smile. "I hope you got some sleep."

"Some." She stared at the table.

"Let me get you some *kaffi* and toast while I make a *gut* breakfast for us."

The old woman frowned at Shelby who was dropping minuscule pieces of cracker on the floor. "How long will that *kind* be here?"

"I told you last night. I'm not sure. I'm sorry

she kept you awake." She went to the stove and pulled a cast-iron frying pan from beneath the oven.

"She doesn't belong here."

"What?" Hannah turned, shocked. *Grossmammi* Ella had always been fond of *kinder*. Many church Sundays, her great-grandmother was the first to volunteer to hold a fussy *boppli* on her lap or watch over a little one so older siblings could join in a game after the service. "She may be my sister."

"I don't believe you! Your *daed* would never cast away his daughter like that."

"He did me." The words came out before she could halt them.

Her *daed* was a sore subject between her and *Grossmammi* Ella. The old woman believed Isaac Lambright would return someday and confess his sins before the congregation. Hannah wondered how her great-grandmother could continue to believe that after fifteen years. Hannah's anger and grief at being left behind herself had been brought to the forefront by Shelby's abandonment.

Dear Lord, show me the way to forgive my daed *as You taught us. I can't find a way in my heart to grant him forgiveness after what he's done.*

"Don't forget what's in God's Ten Command-

ments. A *kind* should honor her *daed* and *mamm*."
Her great-grandmother's scowl deepened.

"Ja." She broke eggs into the frying pan and
took out her frustration on them by stirring them
hard. She did her best to keep the command-
ments, but her *daed*'s selfish actions made re-
specting him difficult.

*I'll try harder, Lord. Help me remember
what's important.* She glanced over her shoulder as Shelby flung out her hands. A shower of
cracker crumbs went everywhere, into the little girl's hair, onto the floor, onto the table…
onto *Grossmammi* Ella who abruptly smiled
and handed the toddler another cracker. That
delighted Shelby who babbled with excitement.

Hannah wanted to wrap her arms around them
both and hold them close. The days to come
wouldn't be easy, but for her family, she'd try
her hardest.

"Komm in, young man," called a wavering
voice when Daniel peeked around the front door
of the Lambrights' house after no one responded
to his knock. "Don't just stand there." The voice
took on a reproving tone. *"Komm* in."

Daniel did, giving his eyes a moment to adjust
to the interior after the bright early morning sunshine. Unbuttoning his coat, he didn't take it off.
He doubted he'd be staying long. He shifted his

hold on the bag holding the shampoo and diapers he'd bought at his brother's store.

A very old woman sat by the window. She was almost gaunt, and her white hair was so thin he could see her scalp through her *kapp*. Her bony fingers looked like talons as she clasped them on her black apron over her dress of the same color. But her eyes drilled through him as if he were a naughty boy standing in front of his teacher.

"I'm Ella Lambright," she said, "but you can call me *Grossmammi* Ella. Who are you?"

"Daniel Stoltzfus."

She eyed him up and down. "You have the look of Paul Stoltzfus about you."

"He was my *daed*."

"No wonder you look like him then. Why are you here? Are you courting our Hannah?"

Before he could reply, he heard a quick intake of breath beyond the old woman. Glancing toward the kitchen, he saw Hannah wiping her hands on a dish towel. Shelby was sitting in a high chair and eating what looked like toast covered with honey. The toddler would need another bath as soon as she was finished, because honey was smeared all over her face.

Hannah flipped the dish towel over the shoulder of her dark purple dress as her gaze locked with his. She didn't move or look away. He found he couldn't either when he saw the deep wells of sorrow in her emotive eyes. Had she believed he'd return with her *daed* this morning? No, she hadn't believed that, but she'd hoped. How could he fault her for her faith that all would turn out well in the end? Now wasn't the time to tell her he'd learned that, though God was a loving Father, He didn't have time to take care of details. Daniel had decided years ago to handle those on his own.

"Gute mariye," he said into the strained silence. Pulling out the shampoo bottle from among the packages of diapers, he added, "My sister-in-law uses this on her *boppli* because it's gentle on little ones' hair and doesn't sting their eyes."

"Danki." Her hand trembled as she took the bag without letting her fingers brush his. Setting it on the counter by the sink, she said nothing when he came into the kitchen.

Shelby stretched out sticky fingers toward him. She began to chatter in nonsense sounds. She bounced on the hard high chair, excited to see him again. Honey dripped off her chin, and bits of bread were glued to her face and her hands.

He kissed the top of her head. "How are you doing, Shelby?"

Giggling, she offered him a tiny piece of toast. He ate it, pretending he was going to eat her fingers, as well. That made her laugh louder. He was astonished how deep and rich the sound was.

The toddler's high spirits vanished when Hannah approached her with a washcloth to clean her hands and face. Shelby screwed up her face and opened her mouth to cry.

Daniel yanked the wet cloth from Hannah's hand. When she protested, he said, "Let me do it. There's no reason to upset her again."

"All right." Resignation filled Hannah's voice.

As he cleaned honey and bread crumbs off the little girl's hands, he stole a glance toward her older sister. He almost gasped aloud at the pain and despair on Hannah's face. Every instinct told him to toss aside the cloth and pull Hannah into his arms and console her. When they were walking out together, he wouldn't have hesitated, but everything was different since the night he decided he had to be single-minded in the pursuit of his dream of running a construction company.

"While you're getting the stickiness off her, I'll get my beekeeping equipment." Her voice was muffled, and he guessed she was struggling to hold back the tears he'd seen in her eyes when she wasn't aware he was looking in her direction.

Again he'd had the chance to say something comforting, but he couldn't think of anything that wouldn't upset her. What a disaster he'd made of what had been a *gut* friendship! To be honest, he was surprised she even talked to him after he'd avoided her during the past three years.

The back door closed behind her, and Daniel focused his attention on Shelby who slapped the high chair tray, getting her fingers sticky again. Picking her up, he sat her on the edge of the table. He succeeded in getting most the honey off her, but some stuck in her hair.

"She's a *gut* girl," said *Grossmammi* Ella from her chair by the window.

"*Ja*, she is." He grinned at Shelby. "And she's washed."

"Not that one! Our Hannah is a *gut* girl."

Daniel wasn't sure what the elderly woman was trying to convey to him. Did she want him to leave her great-granddaughter alone so he didn't have a chance to hurt her again, or was *Grossmammi* Ella hoping he'd court Hannah? He thought about assuring her that he had no plans to do either. Nothing had changed for him. He was working toward his goal, and it required every bit of his attention.

The door opening allowed him to avoid answering the old woman. In astonishment, he saw Hannah was dressed as she'd been when she'd left. Didn't beekeepers wear protective suits to keep from getting stung? She held a small metal container with a spout like an inverted funnel on one side and small bellows on the other. The odor of something burning came from it.

"Is that all you're bringing?" he asked.

"The smoker is all I need."

"What does it do?"

She looked at the container and squirted some smoke into the air between them. "It baffles the bees. The smoke masks the chemical signals bees use to communicate with each other. They can't warn each other I'm near. Otherwise, they'd believe the hive is in danger, and they'd attack. It's an easy way to get close to a hive without getting stung."

"A *gut* idea. I'm not fond of bees."

"They'll leave you alone if you leave them alone."

"But we aren't going to leave them alone." He reached to take Shelby's tiny jacket off a nearby peg. It was bright red, and the front closed with a zipper and was decorated with yellow ducklings, something no plain *kind* would wear.

"What are you doing?" Hannah asked.

"Getting Shelby's coat on her. I'll let you help your great-grandmother."

"What? I'm not taking a toddler or *Grossmammi* Ella near the bees."

"They could stay by the road and—"

"Don't be silly." She pushed past him and strode toward the front door. "You stay here with them, and I'll go to the bridge." Turning, she smiled, and something pleasant—something he remembered from when they spent time together—rippled through him. "I don't need you to point out where the bees are. I can find them." She left.

Daniel went out onto the porch with Shelby in his arms, her coat half on. Behind him, he heard *Grossmammi* Ella asking where everyone was going. He saw her struggling to get to her feet. He didn't hesitate as he rushed back into the house, not wanting the old woman to fall.

Making sure Hannah's great-grandmother was seated again and the door closed, he stared out the window as Hannah stepped over the stone wall beside the guardrail. She hurried down the steep hill toward the creek.

He wasn't worried about her falling in. The current was sluggish because the water behind the dam upstream beside the remnants of the old mill was still partially frozen. Daniel wanted to get as much work as possible done before the water rose when the ice melted. Once the failing joists were replaced, he could complete the interior work even if it rained. Discovering the hive had threatened to destroy his timetable.

He had to make this job a success. The bridge was one of the few in the area not washed away by Hurricane Agnes in 1972. The wear and tear on the bridge couldn't be ignored any longer. The original arched supports and the floor joists needed to be strengthened. Most of the deck boards would have to be replaced. The walls were rotted. Work he knew how to do, and he'd been pleased when the highway supervisor, Jake Botti, asked him to take over the project. It was the first step toward his long-held dream of becoming a general contractor.

Suddenly Shelby began chattering in his ear and wiggling. He set her on the floor. Once he took off her coat, she waddled to a chair and began to try to pull herself onto it.

Daniel's eyes shifted between the toddler and Hannah who was standing by the bridge and staring at the beam where he'd found the bees. She squirted smoke at the opening several times. She paused, then squeezed the bellows on the side of the smoker again. The wisps of smoke swirled around her, making her disappear; then she emerged from the gray cloud and retraced her steps to the house.

He opened the door before she could. "Did you see them?"

"Ja." She left her smoker on the porch, then came into the house. Motioning with her head toward the kitchen, she walked past Shelby who was focused on climbing onto the chair.

Grossmammi Ella didn't acknowledge any

of them as she continued to gaze out the window. Unsure if she'd notice if Shelby fell, Daniel grabbed the toddler before he went into the kitchen.

"Would you like some tea while we talk?" Hannah asked as she opened the cupboard and reached in for two cups.

"Sounds *gut*. I'll put Shelby in her high chair, if you'd like."

She shook her head. "Let her play on the floor. Next to the sewing machine, there's a small box of toys I found in the attic. Will you get them out for her?"

He complied, trying to curb his impatience. He wanted to ask about the bees again. If Hannah couldn't move them, work would have to be delayed until an exterminator could come to the bridge. Having promised he'd get the project done in six weeks or less, losing precious time might make the difference between finishing on time or being late.

Hannah didn't speak again after she'd placed two steaming cups on the table. Sitting, she waited for him to pull out the chair across from her. She took a sip from her cup, then said, "You're right. It's a hive of honeybees."

"Can you move it?"

She nodded as she wrapped her hands around her cup. "I'll have to move it twice."

"Why?"

"If we lived farther away from the bridge, I could move your hive once. Because I keep my own hives so close to the bridge, if I move those new bees to a new hive behind the house, they'll simply return to the bridge and rebuild their hive. I'll keep them in the cellar in the dark for the next couple of weeks or so. Then, when I put the new hive outside, the bees will have lost their scent trails to the bridge. They'll become accustomed to the new location and stay here."

He watched her face as she continued speaking of relocating the bees as if they were as important to her as her great-grandmother. Her voice contained a sense of authority and undeniable knowledge about how to execute her plan. The uncertain girl he'd known three years ago had become a woman who was confident in her ability with bees.

When she smiled, an odd, but delightful tremor rushed through him again. He dampened it. They were in the here and now, not the past.

"Daniel, I'll need you to do one more thing for me as part of our bargain."

"What's that?"

"The hive is going to need a new home. I don't have any extra honey supers, and it will take at least a week or two for some to arrive from my supplier."

"Honey supers?"

"The boxes stacked to make a hive."

He wasn't sure what she was talking about, but he said, "Show me what you need, and I'll build it. Anything else?"

"No. I've got the rest of the materials I need."

When Hannah went to the back door, he scooped up Shelby and followed. Somehow he was going to have to persuade these two stubborn Lambright women they could trust each other. He wasn't sure how.

Daniel faltered as Hannah walked to two stacks of rectangular boxes set off the ground on short legs. She glanced back as if wondering why he'd stopped, but she halted, too, when her gaze settled on Shelby. Hannah explained what size the four stackable boxes she'd need for the new hive must be as well as describing the cross braces that supported the frames for the honeycomb.

"Sounds simple enough," he said when she finished.

A raindrop struck his face, then another. He glanced up as rain pelted them. Together they rushed into the house. Shelby giggled as she bounced in his arms.

Hannah closed the door behind them. "It looks as if the sky is going to open up. You're going to get wet."

If you don't head out now. He finished the rest of her sentence, which she hadn't spoken. She couldn't make it any clearer he was overstaying his welcome.

He'd take the hint, but not until he got the information he needed. "When will you be able to move the bees?"

"It can't be a rainy day or a warm one. The rain can hurt the bees when I cut the comb out of the old hive, and, if it's warm, they'll be flying about looking for nectar. A lot of the bees could be lost that way." She looked past him to where rain splattered on the window over the sink. "As soon as you have the supers built and the weather cooperates, I'll move them. Looks like rain tomorrow, so I can do it the day after if everything's ready."

"Sounds *gut*." He slapped his forehead. "No, day after tomorrow won't work. You've got to take Shelby to Paradise Springs that day."

"What?"

"On my way here, I stopped at the health clinic and made a *doktor*'s appointment for Shelby."

"You did what?" Her brown eyes darkened with strong emotions. "Shelby is my responsibility, not yours."

"*Ja*, but, when I told my *mamm* about finding Shelby, she insisted the *kind* be seen by the *doktorfraa* as soon as possible." He grinned, hoping she'd push aside her anger. "I learned many years ago not to argue with my *mamm* when she speaks with that tone."

Hannah's eyes continued to snap at him, but she took a deep breath and released it as he set the toddler beside the box of toys again. He pulled out the appointment card with the time on it and handed it to her.

In a calmer tone, as she put the card in the pocket of her apron, she said, "I'm sorry. I should have thanked you for making the appointment, Daniel." Before he could relax, she hurried on, "But from this point forward, making appointments for Shelby has to be my responsibility and mine alone. If the note's right, she's my sister. If she's not, she was left on my porch. But I do appreciate your *mamm* being concerned about her. Please tell her."

"I will, and, Hannah, if you'd like, I'll go with you and Shelby to the appointment." He glanced at the *kind*. "I can see she's not cooperating with you."

"That's a *gut* idea."

Surprised at her quick acceptance of his help, when she'd resisted at every turn before, he said, "I'll pick you up about a half hour before the appointment, if that works for you."

"That should be fine."

When she didn't add anything else, he knew

he needed to leave. Something he couldn't name urged him to stay, but he ignored it, unsure what would happen if he lingered an extra minute more.

Ruffling Shelby's hair, he bid Hannah and her great-grandmother goodbye. He heard the toddler cry out in dismay as he closed the door behind him. The sound chased him across the grass and toward his buggy on the road alongside the creek. As he climbed in, a motion inside the house caught his eye.

A shadow moved in front of the living room window. Was Hannah watching him leave? He was surprised when he realized he hoped she was.

He sighed. Hannah Lambright was as unpredictable as the bees she loved, and he was going have to be extra careful around her.

Extra, extra careful.

Chapter Four

Daniel kneaded his lower back as he got to his feet. He'd already worked a full day and had decided to use a few hours after supper to work on his special project. He stretched out kinks and looked around the living room of the house he was building in the woods on his family's farm. Nailing floor molding was a time-consuming job, especially when he wasn't using a nail gun as he did when he worked for *Englisch* contractors. He could have borrowed an air compressor to power his tools, but he'd decided he wanted to build the house as his ancestors had. Now he was paying for his pride.

Hochmut. One of the most despised words among the Amish, because plain folks found pride contemptible. But he'd had a *gut* reason for his decision. He intended to use the house as a showcase for his skills when he solicited clients. He needed to stick with the choice he'd made. His family considered him too frivolous already because he took a different girl home from each singing.

Mamm had mentioned more than once—some days—it was time he considered starting a family as his other brothers were doing. She'd been delighted as each of her *kinder* married. Both of his sisters were wed as well as three of his six brothers, not including Isaiah who was a widower. His oldest brother Joshua remarried last year, surprising Daniel who'd wondered if Joshua would recover from his grief at the death of his first wife.

Leaning one shoulder against the kitchen doorway that needed to be framed, Daniel appraised what else wasn't done. The rest of the molding, painting, appliances in the kitchen, furniture. A year ago, he'd thought the idea of having a showcase for what he could do was an inspired idea, but now he just wanted to be done. Once he had projects completed for clients, he could use them as examples, and he'd give this house to his twin brother, Micah, when he married.

Micah was in love with Katie Kay Lapp, the bishop's daughter, but Katie Kay couldn't know because his twin brother, Micah, hadn't asked to take her home. Not once. Instead, he'd stood aside month after month, mooning over the vivacious young woman while others courted her. That Katie Kay seemed to have no steady suitor had convinced Micah he had a chance with the woman who was at the center of every gathering.

If Micah did get up his gumption and walked out with Katie Kay other than in his imagination, the house in the woods would be the perfect wedding gift. Maybe it was a *gut* thing Micah continued to hesitate because the house was taking longer to finish than Daniel had expected.

On other jobs, Daniel was accustomed to working with a crew. He'd had to do the work of different trades as he poured a foundation, raised walls and put on the roof. When he hadn't known how to run the propane lines to power the refrigerator, the range and the stoves that would heat the cozy house, he'd watched and learned from a plumber at a project where Daniel was doing the roofing. With each unfamiliar task, he was able to correct any mistakes he made on his house, so he wouldn't have to do the same for his clients.

The door opened with a squeak. Daniel added oiling the hinges to his to-do list as his brother Jeremiah walked in.

Like the rest of the Stoltzfus brothers, Jeremiah was tall and unafraid of work. His hair was reddish-brown and a few freckles remained of the multitude that once covered his face and hands. His hands were often discolored with the stain and lacquer he applied to the furniture pieces he built. He wasn't shy, but could never be described as outspoken either. He stayed quiet when he didn't have anything to say.

"You wanted to borrow my miter box," he said in lieu of a greeting. He held out the tool that would allow Daniel to cut the corners for the supers he planned to make for Hannah tonight.

"Danki."

Jeremiah squatted to appraise Daniel's work. "Are you painting the molding white or staining it?"

"I haven't decided." He grinned at his older brother. "I know you'd stain it. You hate painted wood."

"Paint hides the beauty and imperfections in the wood." Glancing over his shoulder, he said, "I hear you're involved with Hannah Lambright again."

"Involved? Not really. I'm helping her take care of a toddler, and she's helping me move a beehive off the bridge."

"That sounds like involvement to me."

Daniel picked up his hammer and moved across the room. Kneeling, he drove another nail into a section of molding. "Not in the way you're insinuating. Hannah treats me as if I'm a necessary evil."

"That can't be a surprise to you."

It wasn't, but he didn't intend to admit that to his brother. Jeremiah was the one who was most like their *daed*. Paul Stoltzfus had been calm, taking each challenge as it came. Jeremiah, on the other hand, was calm almost to the point of appearing passionless for anything but his work. If his brother had recently taken a girl home from a youth gathering, Daniel hadn't heard of it. Jeremiah wouldn't walk out with a girl without planning every detail and considering every ramification. He wouldn't have made the mistakes Daniel had with Hannah.

"I'm pleased," Daniel said, "she can remove the bees. I wasn't looking forward to getting stung." He gestured with his head toward the boards on the far side of the room. "I'm making her a hive, and she'll make sure the bees are out of our way."

Jeremiah didn't say anything for several minutes, and the only sound was the hammer driving nails into the wood.

Daniel waited, knowing his brother must have something else to say if he'd come over to the house.

"When are you seeing her again?" Jeremiah asked as if there hadn't been a break in the conversation.

"I'm seeing her *and* Shelby the day after tomorrow. Shelby has an appointment for a checkup at the clinic in town, and the little girl refuses to cooperate with Hannah."

"And she does with you?"

He gave his brother a wry smile. *"Ja."*

"That doesn't make sense." Jeremiah held up his hands to forestall Daniel's reply. "You don't need to answer. I know what you're going to say. When did any woman, no matter her age, make sense to a man?"

"I wasn't going to say that."

"No?" His brother laughed, at ease in the unfinished house in a way that he wasn't around a crowd of people. "If so, it's the first time you *haven't* said that."

Daniel wanted to shoot back a sharp reply, but he couldn't. Not when Jeremiah was right. He'd said those words more times than he could count. Each time, he'd meant them.

So why wasn't he saying them tonight?

Two reasons: Hannah Lambright and her little sister, Shelby. They'd invaded his thoughts, and he couldn't shake them loose. He shouldn't feel responsible for Shelby because he'd discovered her on the Lambrights' porch, but he did. And, as for Hannah, he shouldn't feel…however he felt. He wasn't sure what to call the morass of emotions bubbling through him whenever he thought of her or spoke with her.

But he was sure of one thing. He needed to get those feelings sorted out before he saw her again.

Hannah sat at the kitchen table and worked on the equipment she'd need for moving the bees. She'd thought about doing a load of laundry before Shelby and her great-grandmother woke, but rain was falling steadily.

She hoped the day after tomorrow would be dry and cool. If the bees on the covered bridge were cold, they'd cling to the center of the hive and be unlikely to swarm. She must prevent a swarm. Once the queen took it in her mind to leave, the rest of the bees would follow. They might fly to the next opening in the boards beneath the bridge. The current hive wasn't difficult for her to reach, but farther out along the bridge would make it impossible. And it must not be raining when she moved the bees. Removing them from the safety of their hive in the rain could mean some drowning in the open super she'd use to carry them away from the bridge.

Reaching for another of the rectangular frames she'd used for the honeycomb, Hannah glanced out the window at her pair of hives farther up the hill toward the stone barn. She didn't keep them close to the house, because *Grossmammi* Ella was scared of being stung.

The bees would start emerging soon. Nothing

was blooming, so they had no work. If the rain stopped and the weather grew sunny, the bees would try to keep busy anyhow. She must make sure they had food in the hive so they wouldn't starve before they could start gathering pollen and nectar.

Looking at the frames on the table in front of her, she smiled. She'd checked each one to make sure it was in *gut* condition. If Daniel made the supers to her specifications, she could hook the pieces of comb onto the frames with rubber bands and set them in the boxes. The bees would take care of the rest, hooking the comb into place.

A piece of mesh was in the center of the table. She'd place it at the bottom of the hive, so debris could fall from the hive out onto the ground. She had everything she needed other than the supers.

Her hands stilled on the stack of frames. Had she been a complete fool to agree to help Daniel in exchange for him teaching her about taking care of Shelby?

Give to him that asketh thee, and from him that would borrow of thee turn not thou away. The verse from Matthew echoed inside her mind.

She'd done the right thing to accept Daniel's suggestion of a barter, but it wasn't easy to see him day after day, because each conversation was another reminder of how he'd dumped her without a backward glance. She appreciated how he'd offered to help her take Shelby to the *doktorfraa*. The *kind* had screamed every time Hannah came near her yesterday until *Grossmammi* Ella had begun to complain. Tears had led to another night with no sleep. Now, her great-grandmother and the toddler were asleep, so Hannah had time to gather what she needed for the bees' removal.

A noise came from upstairs. The sound of Shelby's crib creaking against the floor. The little girl must be awake.

Gathering the frames and mesh, Hannah set them beside her sewing machine. She hurried up the stairs and into the *kind*'s room. A bed draped with a quilt was pushed against the wall to leave room in the middle for the crib Hannah had used as a *boppli*.

For once, the little girl didn't shriek at the sight of her. Instead, she cried silent sobs. Her left cheek was swollen, and she kept pulling at the side of her mouth. When the *kind* started to make her gibberish sounds, Hannah noticed a swelling on her left lower gum.

"Oh, you poor little girl," she murmured. "You're teething, ain't so?"

She cuddled Shelby close with the toddler's right cheek against her shoulder. Carrying her downstairs, she went into the kitchen. She kept Shelby balanced on her hip while opening a cupboard and taking out a bottle of honey.

"Let's try this." She dipped her finger into the open bottle and rubbed a little bit of honey on Shelby's gum.

The *kind* started to pull away, then paused as the sweet flavor soothed her. Or maybe the honey had already eased the pain. Hannah wasn't sure, but Amos Stoltzfus, Daniel's brother who owned the grocery store, had mentioned several times he'd been asked by a *mamm* for honey to help with her *boppli*'s teething.

Carrying the little girl into the living room, Hannah sat in the rocking chair and brushed Shelby's sweaty bangs off her forehead. Hannah crooned a wordless tune as the little girl faded into a deep slumber. For the first time since her arrival at the house, Shelby didn't fight going to sleep.

What a *wunderbaar* bundle the toddler was in her arms! Hannah hadn't realized, at some moment after Daniel had dumped her and her great-grandmother demanded so much of her attention, she'd relinquished the thought of having *kinder*. When she was younger, she'd dreamed of a house filled with a large family. It'd been lonely being an only *kind* when her classmates had had lots of siblings. She'd watched them together and wondered what it would be like to have sisters and brothers. Almost until the day her *mamm* had died, she'd prayed the Lord would bless her family with more *bopplin*. She'd longed to be the older sister, teaching the little ones to walk and to talk and to play.

God had brought Shelby into her life, and it was Hannah's duty to help the toddler learn to become a *gut* member of their community. This special *kind* was already a blessing.

Maybe, after this morning, the little girl would stop crying whenever Hannah was near. If only it could be that easy!

Hopes of Shelby trusting her vanished as soon as the toddler awoke and began crying the moment her eyes opened. She looked away as Hannah stood and went to the kitchen to get the honey to ease the toddler's teething pain.

"The *boppli* sounds hungry," *Grossmammi* Ella said after Hannah had spread the honey on Shelby's gum again. The old woman walked to the stove with a determination Hannah hadn't seen in months. "I'll make her some fried mush. My *kinder* loved it, and my *kins-kinder* loved it more."

"We've been blessed to have you in the kitchen." Hannah stifled a yawn as she set a fussy Shelby in the high chair. The honey seemed to be doing the trick again because the toddler's screeches had eased to soft whimpers. "Do you want me to measure out the cornmeal?"

Her great-grandmother waved aside her suggestion. "If after all these years of cooking for three generations I can't figure out how to much cornmeal to put in for fried mush, I should give up my apron."

Hannah laughed hard, surprising herself. How long had it been since she'd given in to laughter, letting it surge through her and leaving her awash with happiness? She didn't want to know, because it'd been far too long.

As she worked side by side with her great-grandmother as she'd done since she was ten, she reveled in the simple joys of being with her beloved *Grossmammi* Ella when the old woman's mind was in the present instead of lost in the past. Seeing the twinkle in her great-grandmother's eyes when *Grossmammi* Ella put a piece of fried mush in front of Shelby, Hannah drizzled honey on top of the serving. Not only should the sweetness delight the *kind*, but the additional honey might coat her gum and keep her pain away.

"Look at her eat!" *Grossmammi* Ella crowed as she brought two more servings of delicious fried cornbread to the table. "I told you she was hungry."

"So you did." Hannah's smile broadened. "I appreciate your making breakfast."

"That's kind of you to say, Saloma."

As her great-grandmother began to pour honey

on her fried mush, Hannah turned away. She didn't want *Grossmammi* Ella to see her smile vanish. Saloma was Hannah's *mamm*. Addressing Hannah by her *mamm*'s name was a sign the old woman was slipping away into her memories of the past.

The blessed moments of being a family, something Hannah realized she hadn't treasured enough when she was part of them, came less and less often. Her hope *Grossmammi* Ella would return to the present faded as the meal went on and her great-grandmother continued to call her Saloma.

Though the fried cornmeal probably was delicious, it tasted like grit in Hannah's mouth. Somehow, she forced it down. When her great-grandmother was finished, Hannah assisted her to the chair by the window in the living room.

A quick knock was answered, before Hannah could react, by *Grossmammi* Ella calling, "*Komm* in!"

When Daniel walked in, Hannah's breath caught. Why did he have to be so handsome? Even the cleft in his chin, which she knew he loathed, eased the stark line of his jaw. His ebony hair and bright blue eyes had held her attention from the first time she'd seen him. However, his hands fascinated her. Work-hardened, his broad fingers were gentle on the reins and one time he'd squeezed her hand out of everyone else's sight. Her skin tingled at the memory of the night when she'd dared to believe she'd found the love of her life.

The night before everything had fallen apart...

She pushed aside thoughts of the past and wondered again how her great-grandmother could prefer what had been to what was. Raising her chin, she asked, "Daniel, what are you doing here today? Shelby's appointment at the clinic isn't until tomorrow."

"I know. I came because I brought along the supers you need and—" Past the open door came the rattle of buggy wheels followed by a car door slamming.

From her chair by the window, *Grossmammi* Ella crowed, "Here comes the bishop! Hurry, Hannah! Put on the *kaffi* pot and get out some cookies. You know Reuben has a sweet tooth." She paused and asked in a sharper tone, "Who is that man with him?"

Hannah drew in a sharp breath. A car with *Paradise Springs Police Department* painted on the door was parked in front of the house.

Cold sank through her as the door opened again, but she bit her lip to keep from letting her dismay erupt. The *Englisch* chief of police entered the house with Reuben Lapp. She'd seen

Steven McMurray at auctions and other events, but had never spoken to him.

After leaving his hat on the newel post at the bottom of the stairs, the chief of police greeted her and her great-grandmother with a kind smile. He was out of place in a plain home with his uniform of a dark blue shirt and black pants and shiny badge. The room abruptly seemed too full with the bishop and two tall, muscular men in it.

"I prayed on the matter," Reuben said, "and I feel the right decision is to ask for help from the police to find your *daed*. I hope you agree, Hannah."

Instead of answering, she motioned toward the kitchen. "Would you like to meet Shelby? She's finishing her breakfast."

"Do you think it'll frighten her if we all go into the kitchen?" Reuben asked.

"I don't know." Her smile wobbled. "She doesn't know us."

Her words were contradicted when Shelby gave an excited squeal and held her arms out to Daniel. She began babbling as if she believed he could understand every sound she made.

He walked over to the high chair. "Are you enjoying your breakfast, *liebling*?"

"You called her *liebling*," *Grossmammi* Ella said softly. "That's what my husband called me."

Chief McMurray smiled again at her great-grandmother before he said, "I'm assuming this is Shelby."

At her name, the little girl looked toward him with wide eyes.

"Hello there, Shelby." The big man sat beside the toddler, so he wasn't towering over her.

Hannah couldn't help being impressed at how the policeman spoke quietly and kept a smile on his face. He was making every effort to keep the little girl calm.

But why was the *kind* who might be her little sister smiling at a stranger when she recoiled from Hannah?

Shelby offered a tiny piece of the cornmeal mush to the chief of police.

He took it and pretended to eat it. "*Danki.*"

Shelby tipped her head to one side in obvious bafflement.

"Thank you, Shelby," the police chief said before half turning toward Hannah. "She doesn't understand *Deitsch*?"

"I don't think so," she said. "I don't know if my *daed* speaks it to her. He didn't say in his note."

"I'd appreciate seeing that note. The basket, too."

"I'll get them." She hurried upstairs to Shelby's room and opened the closet. Checking the wrinkled note was in the basket, she carried them downstairs. She wasn't surprised *Grossmammi* Ella had joined the others in the kitchen. Her great-grandmother wouldn't want to miss the excitement.

Hannah set the basket and the note on the table before edging away as Shelby screwed her face to cry again. Why couldn't the *kind* smile at her as she did at everyone else?

Reuben sat beside the policeman as Chief McMurray examined the basket and read the note. When the policeman handed it to him, the bishop scanned it.

"I'd say your *daed*, if he wrote that note, is a man of few words." Chief McMurray watched Shelby try to unstick a dab of honey from the tray. "It'd be easier if she could tell us something." Taking a deep breath, he asked, "Are you willing to take care of her, Hannah?"

"*Ja*. If the note is true, she's my sister."

Grossmammi Ella snorted. "Impossible! Isaac wouldn't treat another daughter like that." She looked at Hannah and quickly away.

"Maybe not," replied Chief McMurray, "but I'm going to act as if it's the truth. Shelby appears to be doing well, and it'd be a pity to bring social services in at this point or put the two of you through a DNA test. I assume you agree, Reuben, leaving the little girl here while we try to find Isaac Lambright is the best solution."

"I do. The *kind* has endured enough already."
The bishop smiled. "And Psalm 127 tells us
kinder are a heritage of the Lord. Shelby is a
gift, and our whole community will help take
care of her."

Chief McMurray stood. "I have no doubts,
which is why I'm leaving her for now with the
Lambrights. In the meantime, I'll start seeing
what I can find out about the missing Isaac Lambright."

"So he can tell you," *Grossmammi* Ella said,
"you're making a big mistake by believing he
could leave another daughter behind. I know he's
under the *bann*, Reuben, but my grandson is a
gut man."

Reuben's voice was conciliatory. "I believe he
is."

"Then why did you bring an *Englisch* policeman here?" She left without a further word.

Hannah started to apologize, but Chief
McMurray halted her.

"I've got an eccentric grandmother myself, so
I understand." He rubbed his chin and sighed.
"It'd help if we had a picture of Isaac, but I know
you don't have one."

"But," Hannah said, "he has to have a license
to drive a car, ain't so? Don't drivers' licenses
have pictures on them?"

The police chief smiled. "I keep forgetting he

doesn't live a plain life now. I'll start a search in the databases. If he has—or has had—a license, he should pop up."

Not quite sure what he meant by *pop up*, Hannah didn't say anything when he offered Reuben a ride to his farm, which the bishop accepted.

Before he left, Reuben prayed with them. "Lord, bless Hannah, Ella and Daniel for opening their hearts to this lost *kind*. Let us not forget how our dear Lord said, *Suffer the little children, and forbid them not, to come unto Me: for of such is the kingdom of Heaven.* We pray that the peace and love of Your kingdom be upon this house and this family. Amen."

Hannah heard Daniel and Chief McMurray echo her "Amen" before the policeman went with the bishop to the front door. The door closed, leaving her in the kitchen with Shelby and Daniel, who'd been oddly quiet.

"How are you doing?" he asked, his eyes clouded with strong emotions.

"Tired." She sighed. "I can tell you there's nothing wrong with her lungs. They get lots of exercise whenever I'm near." Going to the sink, she drew out a clean dishcloth and soaked it. She wrung it out before carrying it to Shelby, intending to wash the *kind*'s hands.

The little girl pulled away with a plaintive cry.

"Let me," Daniel said.

Without a word, Hannah relinquished the cloth when Daniel held out his hand. As he washed Shelby's fingers, he said, "I'm sure it'll get better."

"I wish I could believe that."

"I can stop back later to play with her, if you want."

"Don't you have work on the bridge?"

He shook his head. "The road crew is going to move barriers into place on either side of the bridge today, so we have to stay away. I'd be glad to help here."

"We'll manage," she said as she took the cloth from him and turned toward the sink.

He didn't reply, and she sensed rather than saw his hand stretch out toward her. She held her breath. As shaky as her emotions were, if his fingers settled on her shoulder, she might change her mind about being able to handle the changes in her life. If she let Daniel into her life again and came to depend on him remaining in it, even as a friend, she was opening herself to heartbreak again.

His hand drew back, and she was startled by how her relief was mixed with disappointment. Had she lost her mind? She should be grateful he hadn't touched her. If he had, she feared she would have whirled and thrown herself into his arms. She couldn't do that.

Not now.

Not ever.

Chapter Five

The Hunter's Mill Creek covered bridge sat empty between the concrete barriers that had been set into place to keep vehicles from crossing it. Water had gathered in puddles near the entrance where wooden deck boards had been dented by years of traffic.

Daniel gazed at the bridge as he drove past it. He couldn't wait to get started. Except for one guy, he'd worked with everyone on his five-man crew before and knew they'd do their best on the job. The one person he'd hadn't worked with was the county supervisor's son, and the teenager was using the job to fulfill his volunteering requirement for high school graduation.

A motion caught Daniel's eyes, and he looked at the Lambrights' house. As he turned his horse Taffy toward it, he realized how he'd been avoiding glancing at the house. The questions Jeremiah had asked him the night before last resonated through his head. But no answers did.

I need Your guidance to help make sure I don't hurt Hannah again, Lord.

He repeated the prayer as he drew his buggy to a stop in front of the Lambrights' house. The door opened. He was surprised when only Hannah and an obviously angry Shelby came out. Shelby was dressed, for the first time, in at least some plain clothes. Beneath the coat she'd had with her in the basket, she wore a navy blue dress and white pinafore with her dark socks. Her shoes were still a garish pink. She looked adorable.

But Daniel frowned. Where was her—their great-grandmother?

Unlatching the door on the passenger side as they approached, he shoved it aside. He held out his hands for Shelby who beamed as she caught sight of him. Her stiffness softened when he lifted her from Hannah's arms. Murmuring to the toddler, he saw the hopelessness in her sister's eyes. He tried to imagine his younger sister Esther acting as Shelby did when she was a *boppli* and refusing to have anything to do with him. He would have been heartsick...as Hannah was.

Daniel set the toddler on his lap as Hannah climbed into the buggy and shut the door. Her black bonnet made her hair look like spun gold and her brown eyes darker. But he couldn't help noticing the gray arcs under her eyes.

"Did Shelby stay awake with teething pain?" he asked.

"No. She slept, but *Grossmammi* Ella had a tough night. She can't stop thinking about what my *daed* has done, but she refuses to believe it." She clasped her hands on her lap. "She kept me up all night insisting her grandson was a *gut* man." She grimaced. "More than you wanted to know, I'm sure."

He struggled not to smile. Her expression matched Shelby's when the little girl tasted something she didn't like. "Is *Grossmammi* Ella coming with us?"

Hannah shook her head. "Barry Jones is here." She pointed to the small ranch house farther along the creek road. "He and his family live over there and farm the pastures across the road. He keeps an eye on *Grossmammi* Ella when I have to be away, and she doesn't want to go. He thinks she's amusing, and she thinks he's okay... for an *Englischer*." A faint laugh slipped out. "Those are her exact words, 'He's okay...for an *Englischer*.'"

"I guess I'd better not ask what your great-grandmother says about me."

Hannah's eyes began to twinkle again. "A wise decision."

"Is it so bad?"

"Possibly." She tilted her head toward him and smiled. "Or maybe it isn't bad, and you'd be in danger of a swelled head."

"Ouch!"

Shelby gasped and patted his arm, concern on her face.

Daniel tried again not to laugh, but it was impossible when Hannah was smothering a giggle behind her hand. "I'm fine, *liebling*," he assured the little girl. "I've got to remember how literally they take everything at this age."

"She seems to understand a lot."

"I agree." He shifted the toddler onto the seat between them.

"As irritable as this little one has been today, it's for the best that my great-grandmother didn't want to come along."

"Dealing with one stubborn Lambright woman at a time is enough, ain't so?" His smile faltered when Hannah glowered at him as Shelby tried to crawl onto his lap. Now he'd done it! He'd hoped to make her feel better about Shelby's continuing antagonism toward her. Instead she must have assumed he meant Hannah was the stubborn one. In truth, she could be as obstinate as her great-grandmother or little sister, but he'd wanted to make her smile, not feel worse.

Not the best way to start the day.

"I don't mind holding her," Daniel said.

Another mistake, he realized, when the *kind* smiled and relaxed against him as soon as she sat on his knee again. Beside him, Hannah's expression went as quickly from vexed to hurt.

Help me help her, he prayed, though in his heart, he knew she'd mistrust everything he did until he proved to her that he wasn't the careless young man he'd been when they were walking out. He didn't know how to convince her.

Hannah turned the last page in the stack of papers requesting information about Shelby's health history. It hadn't taken long to fill them out because she knew nothing about Shelby's *mamm*'s pregnancy or health history. As for her *daed*'s, Hannah didn't know much about him either. She'd been too young to ask about such things before he left.

Rising to carry the clipboard to the front desk at the Paradise Springs Health Center, she glanced at Daniel and Shelby. The toddler was giggling as he played another game of peekaboo with her. She hadn't heard Shelby laugh since... Well, since the last time Daniel had come to the house.

The two of them looked as if they belonged together. How sad that after years of wishing for a sibling, she got one who despised her!

Hannah walked to the blue plastic chair that was set against the wall like the others along both sides of the waiting room. It was a comfortable space with light brown carpet and sheer curtains on the pair of windows overlooking Route 30, the road that bisected Paradise Springs. Two other people waited to see the *doktorfraa*. The elderly man was sneezing, and a younger man was coughing and blowing his nose. She hoped whatever they had wasn't contagious. The only thing she could imagine worse than having a toddler who cried whenever she came near was having a *sick* toddler who cried whenever she came near.

As she sat, Hannah picked up a magazine, shuffling the pages. Her attempts to read were stymied each time the little girl chortled with delight. She should be grateful that Daniel entertained Shelby, but she couldn't help wondering what would happen when the bridge project was finished and Daniel didn't visit any longer. She didn't want Shelby hurt as she'd been when his attention had turned from her to other young women.

"Shelby Lambright?" called a nurse from a nearby doorway.

"Here." Hannah jumped to her feet. She reached for the *kind*, but Shelby threw her arms around Daniel's neck.

"I can go with you if you don't mind," he said, glancing around the room.

Knowing he didn't want to make a scene, Hannah nodded. She followed him along a short hallway.

When the nurse went into a room to the right, she smiled at them. "You two have an adorable little girl," the nurse said after checking Shelby's height and weight.

"Danki," Hannah said at the same time as Daniel did. When she glanced at him, he looked away, but she noticed the tops of his ears were red. She wanted to ask why. Now wasn't the time.

Following the instructions the nurse gave before leaving, he set Shelby on the paper-topped examination table. He stepped aside while Hannah undressed the *kind* until she wore only her diaper.

The door reopened, and a slender redhead walked in. Dr. Montgomery wore her stethoscope around her neck and an open white lab coat. She was carrying a manila file. Smiling, she said, "Hello, Hannah. Is this Shelby?"

"Ja," Hannah replied to the doctor who oversaw *Grossmammi* Ella's care. "She's my little sister."

The *doktorfraa* glanced at Daniel.

He cleared his throat and said, "I found Shelby on the front porch at the Lambrights' house."

Dr. Montgomery's brows arched high. "You're going to have to give me a lot more information."

Hannah shared an abridged version of the events earlier in the week. If the *doktorfraa* was shocked, no sign of it was visible on her face. She opened the file and began to read.

Dr. Montgomery's professional smile vanished when she looked up from the sheaf of papers. "Is this the only medical history you have for her? It's nothing."

"I know," Hannah said. "I don't know much about my parents because I was young when my *mamm* died and my *daed* left. And Shelby has a different *mamm*."

"Do you know whether she's been immunized?"

"No."

The *doktorfraa* sighed. "I guess the best thing to do is examine her and determine how she's doing. We'll use today as the baseline and build her medical history from this point forward. But as far as her immunizations, my recommendation is we start them all over again as if she were a newborn."

"That's safe?" Daniel asked.

"Much safer than taking the chance of her not having the full complement. This way, she won't get sick from something that can be prevented." She turned to Hannah. "Do you agree?"

Shock riveted her. The question was a stark

reminder of how Shelby's life would be affected by every decision Hannah made. Hannah had to be more than sister to the little girl. In so many ways, she was going to have to be Shelby's *mamm*, too.

"I want what is best for her," she replied.

Dr. Montgomery nodded, put down the file and asked Hannah to lift Shelby to the floor. Hannah did, releasing the *kind* the moment Shelby was steady on her feet. Having the *doktorfraa* see how the toddler cried if Hannah stayed close too long would create questions she wanted to avoid answering…because she had no answer.

Shelby seemed to think the examination was a game. Dr. Montgomery pulled a dog puppet from her coat pocket and used it to talk to Shelby. The little girl giggled, excited, as she obeyed requests to walk and take a small ball from the *doktorfraa*.

Hannah set the toddler back on the table while Dr. Montgomery scribbled some notes on the page.

"I'd say your guess she's about a year-and-a-half old is accurate," said the *doktorfraa*. "Shelby can walk, though she's a bit wobbly. She recognizes her name, and it appears she's trying to repeat sounds she hears. Those are skills most children with Down syndrome should have mastered by 18 months." She pulled a handheld computer out of her other pocket. Tapping it, she paused to read something on its screen. "Is she able to suck through a straw?"

"Ja," Hannah replied.

"Does she know your names and her own?"

"She knows her own. I'm not sure about ours."

The *doktorfraa* smiled as she raised her stethoscope and blew on it. "We can't expect too much when she's been with you a few days. She recognizes people after they leave the room?"

"Ja."

"Good."

The room grew silent while Dr. Montgomery listened to Shelby's heart, then let the *kind* hear her own heartbeat through the stethoscope. While Shelby was preoccupied, Dr. Montgomery checked her ears, throat and eyes. The little girl giggled when her stomach was palpitated.

"Ticklish, aren't you?" Dr. Montgomery said.

Shelby giggled more, and Hannah heard Daniel smother a chuckle from where he sat at the side of the room. She knew envy was wrong, but she couldn't help wishing again she had the connection with her little sister that he did. Except when Hannah rocked her to sleep, Shelby tolerated her if nobody else was around. Nothing more.

Straightening, the *doktorfraa* said, "Her heart sounds excellent, which is good news. So many children with Down Syndrome have heart issues." She smiled at Shelby who grinned. "However, I saw some signs of frequent ear infections. Those can lead to a hearing loss. Have you noticed she's having trouble hearing?"

"She hears everything," Hannah said with a smile. "Not only in the house, but outside. Whenever a truck goes past, she rushes to look out." Hesitating, she knew it would be unwise not to share everything with the *doktorfraa*. "I think it's because *Daed* may have been driving a truck when he left her at our house."

"So she's looking for him?" Dr. Montgomery's easy smile vanished. "Poor little munchkin. It's hard enough to think of an adult being dropped into a new life without an explanation, but it's got to be more difficult for a toddler who can't understand why. I'm glad that she has you and your great-grandmother, Hannah."

"She's unsure around us." Honesty forced her to add, "Around me especially."

"Give her time. She's known you less than a week." Dr. Montgomery's smile widened. "Young children are eager to love anyone who treats them with kindness. Shelby has lost everything and everyone she's known, so she needs time to adjust. I suspect you'll see great changes in her over the next few weeks. Shelby may come to believe she was blessed the day she was left on your porch." She grinned as Shelby turned a tongue depressor over and over in her hands, examining every bit of it. "A child with Shelby's challenges is welcomed as a gift from God among you plain people."

"She *is* a gift," Hannah said, watching as Shelby began to gnaw on the wooden stick, concentrating on the area where her tooth was coming in. "A special gift."

The *doktorfraa* ran gentle fingers over Shelby's silken hair. "Her disabilities, though we can't know the scope of them at her age, can be met now with physical therapy and occupational therapy."

"Isn't she young to worry about what she'll do when she grows up?" asked Daniel.

"I'm sorry," Dr. Montgomery said, puzzled. "What did you say?"

He looked at Hannah who was glad he'd asked the question she'd been thinking. She motioned for him to go ahead, and he said, "I'm wondering why she needs to worry about an occupation when she's barely more than a *boppli*."

The *doktorfraa* smiled. "Occupational therapy isn't about getting a job. It's about helping Shelby strengthen the physical function she has. Learning fine motor skills and eye-hand coordination."

"Isn't that physical therapy?" Hannah asked,

keeping a hand against Shelby's back so the little girl didn't tumble off the table.

"Physical therapy—or PT, as we call it—is used to help a patient deal with injuries or weaknesses to the muscles." She chuckled. "Don't worry. You'll learn the difference. Most patients and their families confuse the two at first. However, the therapists know their fields well, and they'll help Shelby. In addition, I'd like to have her evaluated to determine how much speech therapy she'll need. Does she speak any words?"

"No, though she makes a lot of different sounds and seems to believe we should understand what she means." Hannah chuckled. "And she's training us well because we're beginning to figure out what she means with some of the sounds."

"Excellent." The *doktorfraa* made some more notes, then said, "All that's needed is her first round of shots." She picked up a folder from the cabinet at one side of the room. "The schedule for childhood shots is listed here as well as information on how most children react to the shots."

Hannah took it. When her little sister cried as she was given several shots, Hannah's attempts to comfort her as she re-dressed the toddler were futile. Shelby continued to cry as Dr. Montgomery handed her a sticker and told her she was a brave and *gut* girl.

The tears stopped when Daniel put the sticker

on her white pinafore. Shelby kept gazing at the bright red kitten. Babbling, she giggled when he pretended to pet the cartoon cat. The toddler kept touching it while Hannah carried her to Daniel's buggy, but began to whimper and suck her thumb as soon as they were seated. Before they left the parking lot, the little girl had fallen into a fitful sleep on Hannah's lap.

"*Danki*, Daniel, for coming with us today," Hannah said beneath the rumble of rain that fell in big, oily drops that sounded like acorns dropping onto the roof of the buggy.

"I told you I'd help you when I could."

"I know, but I wanted to thank you." She let her gaze follow the stern line of his profile as he steered the buggy through the heavy rain. "Won't you accept my gratitude?"

"I don't like being obligated."

"I know, Daniel. I probably know that better than anyone."

He looked away from the road, letting his horse follow it toward the covered bridge and her house. "You do, don't you?"

Instead of the vexation she'd expected, sorrow billowed through her. "I'm trying to leave the past in the past while we work together."

"I know, and you're doing a better job than I am."

"I wouldn't say that."

The faint shadow of a grin played along his volatile lips. "Trust me, Hannah. You are. Will it be okay if I come to watch the little one's first session with the physical therapist?"

She appreciated him not using Shelby's name. That might wake the toddler. "If you want to. You don't have to feel obligated."

"Ouch!" He put his hand to the center of his chest and leaned against the side of the buggy. "I didn't realize how painful it would be to have my own words thrown back at me."

"I didn't mean—" She halted herself when he laughed quietly. Rolling her eyes, she smiled. "Let's talk about something else."

"A *wunderbaar* idea! Are you planning to move the bees tomorrow?"

"If it's not raining."

"*Gut.* I'll let my crew know they should plan to come to the bridge the following morning." He rested his elbows on his knees. "What time do you plan to move them?"

"Just before sunset. The air is chilly then, so the bees will be less active. However, I want to make sure I've got plenty of light so I can find the queen among the layers of honeycombs. Without her making the transfer, it'll be for nothing. The rest of the bees will desert their new hive."

"How long should it take?"

"If all goes well, I'll be done by dark, but I

don't want to make promises. There can be complications moving any hive."

"What can I do to help?"

"Watch Shelby and *Grossmammi* Ella while I'm at the bridge."

"I'd like to see the process of moving the bees. Not that I want to get close to them. You seem to trust them, but I don't. So I'd like to watch from a safe distance."

She shook her head. "I need you to stay away and keep everyone else away. If the bees get spooked, they'll go on the defensive. I don't want to get stung any more than necessary."

He stiffened and looked at her. "You'll get stung moving them?"

"Getting stung is always a possibility when working with bees. Even with the precautions I take, I can't be sure what might set them off. If I was afraid of being stung, I couldn't be a beekeeper." She shrugged. "Besides, I'm accustomed to it."

"I don't like the idea of you getting hurt." His hands tightened on the reins. "I shouldn't have asked you to move the bees."

"If I didn't do it, you'd have to kill the hive. That would be a real tragedy." She started to put her hand out to touch his arm to emphasize her point, but pretended she was adjusting her hold on Shelby. Touching him, even chastely, would be stupid. She needed to keep the barrier between them, the barrier made brick by brick by his betrayal and the indifference that followed.

But it was becoming more difficult every day to reconcile the man he was now with the one he'd been then.

Chapter Six

The most recent rainstorm had stopped by the time Daniel got out of his buggy at the Lambrights' house. Every day for the past week, except yesterday, there had been a downpour around midday or it'd rained all day. Not a heavy rain, but enough to make the air cold and clammy.

Taffy shook his mane, scattering water in every direction.

Patting the horse on the neck, Daniel said, "I know. I'm looking forward to a dry day, too."

The horse regarded him with a skeptical glance as if to remind Daniel that Taffy would remain out in the storm while Daniel went inside the dry house.

"I'll make it up to you, old boy," he said with a chuckle. "*Mamm* has a few apples left in the cellar."

Pricking his ears forward at the mention of his

favorite treat, Taffy bowed his head in a pose of acceptance.

Again Daniel laughed as he lifted the new supers he'd built for Hannah out of the back of his buggy. The horse had a way of making himself understood without uttering a single word.

He wished it was as easy to know what Hannah was thinking. Or maybe he was trying to ignore the truth in front of him. She didn't hide that she cared about Shelby, though the toddler pulled away from her. He wished he could figure out why the little girl reacted that way. Hannah treated her with every kindness and made certain she had foods she liked.

Taking the porch steps in two leaps, Daniel set the supers down before he walked toward the door. It opened as he reached it.

Grossmammi Ella stood in the doorway, her black dress contrasting with her white *kapp.* "*Komm* in. Why are you standing on the porch, Earney?"

Daniel glanced over his shoulder, wondering if someone else stood behind him. No, he was the only one on the porch. Whom was *Grossmammi* Ella talking to? Or to whom did she *think* she was talking? Reuben had said something about the old woman losing her way. Was this what the bishop had meant? She'd acted odd before, but nothing like this.

Keeping his voice even, he began, "*Grossmammi* Ella—"

She laughed. "Don't you start calling me that, Earney. That's for our *kins-kinder*, not for old folks like us."

What was going on? She spoke as if she and he were the same age. And *Grossmammi* Ella grinned at him in a way that brought Shelby to mind. Innocent and eager and filled with delight at seeing him. It was almost as if she'd become a *kind* again.

When she urged him again to enter, he did. The hiss of a propane lamp could be heard beneath Shelby's soft singsong words from where she was playing beside her great-grandmother's chair. She had a cloth book open on her lap and was turning the pages. When Daniel moved closer to the *kind*, he realized the pictures were upside down.

Where was Hannah? She must be close. She wouldn't leave *Grossmammi* Ella and Shelby for long. But when he looked into the kitchen, he didn't see her.

He started to ask where Hannah was, but the old woman interrupted him. "Do you want some *kaffi*? I'll brew it extra strong because I know how you like it dark, Earney."

Daniel struggled to hide his uneasiness. *Gross-*

mammi Ella thought he was someone else. Who was Earney?

"Regular strength is fine," he replied with care. He wasn't sure which word might cause her to say something else strange. As much as the old woman's hands shook, he doubted she should be handling the *kaffi* pot. She could scald herself. "I'll get it."

"Making *kaffi* isn't a man's job. It's his wife's job and her joy," she replied, turning toward the kitchen so fast she stumbled.

He caught her arm before she could fall on Shelby. Urging her to stay where she was, he assured her that he'd changed his mind about the *kaffi*.

Where was Hannah?

The back door opened, and Hannah came in. He was astonished at the outfit she was wearing. A mesh screen beneath a broad white head cover protected her face but allowed her to see. Her loose, white coat reached over white trousers that covered her legs and vanished into boots closed with rubber bands. She carried leather gloves with extra long cuffs in one hand and her smoker in the other. Over her shoulder was a canvas bag with what looked like picture frames stuffed into it.

A long sigh emerged from *Grossmammi* Ella when Hannah walked toward them, and she seemed to shrink as he watched. She hunched over as if the weight of her years had descended on her shoulders. When she teetered, he took her thin arm and guided her to the chair by the window. She looked away from him and out at the setting sun visible beneath the thick bank of clouds.

Tiny arms grabbed his leg, and he saw Shelby grinning at him. She bounced on her bottom, every inch of her bristling with excitement.

He bent and kissed her head. "What mischief are you up to today, *liebling*?" Scooping her up, he carried her into the kitchen.

He was amazed when Hannah didn't take off the helmet as he spoke. He couldn't see her face clearly beneath the veil as he asked, "Who's Earney?"

"Earney was *Grossmammi* Ella's husband. Earnest Lambright. He died almost thirty years ago." Puzzlement filled her voice. "Why are you asking about him?"

"Your great-grandmother was talking to me as if she believed I was him."

"What?" Even with the hat and veil in place, he could hear her shock.

"She called me by his name when I came to the door. At first, I thought she was mistaken because it's cloudy and the light's not *gut*. Now I'm not sure."

"She gets mixed up sometimes. The problem is her mind is so full of memories she gets them confused."

"What does the *doktor* say?"

Instead of answering him, Hannah said, "I need to get started if I want to be done before it gets dark again."

"What can I do to help?" he asked, knowing that pressing her for more answers would be useless.

"Like I told you before, you can help me best by staying here with *Grossmammi* Ella and keeping an eye on Shelby."

He frowned. "My horse Taffy is out front. Will he be in danger?"

"Not if everything goes as it should. But if you want to bring him around back, go ahead."

He considered for a moment, then shook his head. "I'm sure you'll keep the situation under control."

"*Ja*, because before the bees would have a chance to sting Taffy, they'd be stinging me."

"That's incentive enough for anyone."

She chuckled, the sound distorted by the veiling. "Now you understand."

Though he was tempted to say he didn't understand much of what was going on in the house, he asked, "Are you sure there's nothing else I can do?"

"Knowing someone is watching over *Gross-mammi* Ella and Shelby will allow me to concentrate on moving the bees." She pulled on one glove, making sure the long cuff was drawn up beneath the elastic at the hem of her sleeve. That way, he realized, no honeybee could crawl under her protective clothing. "Did you bring the supers?"

"They're on the porch. I also brought along a hand truck for you to use to get the boxes to the house once you've got the bees in them. I wasn't sure if you'd want to bring them all at once or not, but I left the hand truck by the bridge."

"Let's take it one step at a time."

"And the steps are…?"

"First I'll smoke the bees. When they're dazed, I'll cut each section of the comb out and attach it to a frame with rubber bands. The frames go into the supers, which I'll put in the cellar. I'd better get started."

When she walked past him, he caught her arm as he had her great-grandmother. He was shocked when something that felt like the buzz from a thousand bees rushed from where his fingertips touched her. It'd never happened before, not even when he was taking her home in his buggy.

He heard her sharp gasp. Had she felt the strange sensation, too?

He wanted to ask her that…and so many other

things, things he couldn't put into words. *Don't be foolish again*! came the warning from his conscience. To speak of unexplored feelings could lead to her believing his priorities had changed. They hadn't. He had to focus on building his construction company.

"Daniel?" she asked, her voice trembling.

He lifted his hand off her arm. "I wanted to tell you to be careful."

"You don't have to. I know to be careful." She strode away.

He started to put Shelby in her high chair so he could give her a cookie, but halted and turned to look at the closing door. Had she been talking about the bees when she spoke of being careful? A boulder dropped through his stomach as he wondered if she'd been talking about him instead. That thought bothered him more than it should.

And that bothered him even more.

Hannah puffed smoke at the bees. Already they were quieting in the massive hive within the timbers beneath the bridge. Once they were dazed enough, she'd begin removing the layers of honeycomb and transfer them to the frames. Most of the bees would cling to the comb during the transfer. The rest would fall onto the white sheet she'd spread out next to one super. Seeing the entrance, they'd crawl in and join the rest of the members of the hive.

Once she found the queen bee, she'd put her into the bee carrier along with a couple of her worker bee attendants. The queen was vital to making the transfer a success, so when Hannah saw the bee that was a giant in comparison with the others, she smiled...and then winced.

Ach! Her left cheek ached from where *Grossmammi* Ella had struck her before breakfast. The shock of having her gentle, warmhearted great-grandmother lash out with abrupt fury hurt more than the impact of the old woman's hand.

Grossmammi Ella had been on edge since the bishop and Chief McMurray had come to the house a few days ago. She'd refused to sit at the table for meals, insisting she eat in her room where she felt safe, and she fussed every time Shelby did. Last night before bedtime, her eyes had flashed with the first sparks of a temper she'd never shown during the years Hannah was growing up. She'd been infuriated when Shelby woke in the middle of the night and had snarled at Hannah to make sure the *boppli* was quiet.

Hannah had recognized the signs of an impending storm, but she hadn't expected it to explode from her great-grandmother before they ate breakfast. Hannah had avoided the worst of the blow, but the impact had been enough to leave a red blotch on her face hours later.

She'd seen Daniel's curiosity about why she hadn't removed her hat and veil. She didn't want to answer the questions he was certain to ask if he saw the mark on her face. Those questions could lead to more, including if Hannah was capable of taking care of her great-grandmother.

Capturing the queen bee and two other bees close to her, Hannah shut them into the small plastic box built for this purpose. She then continued moving comb into the frames and sliding them into the supers, but her thoughts weren't on her work.

Would her great-grandmother be taken away if others discovered the truth of their situation? Was it safe for Shelby to be in the house with the old woman? The *Englisch* police wouldn't be willing to leave the little girl in what they deemed a dangerous place.

Should she speak with Reuben? She didn't want to think her bishop would insist she relinquish Shelby to another's care.

In spite of her determination not to, as she removed the last piece of comb and secured it, she glanced toward the house. Daniel stood by the front window with Shelby clinging again to him. His broad hand was around the *kind*, but his gaze was fixed on Hannah. Concern drew his mouth into a straight line.

She wanted to believe he was anxious for her safety. Once upon a time, when Daniel had first walked out with her—or at least, she'd believed he was walking out with her—she would have been certain his trepidation was for her. She wasn't sure what to think.

Setting one super on top of another, she put a board on the upper one. She did the same with the other supers. Noticing no bees were visible on the sheet, she picked up one pair of supers and began walking up the hill toward the road. She set them on the hand truck before collecting the others. Within minutes, she'd gathered her equipment and the sheet.

Hannah was glad, when she approached the house, that Daniel hadn't brought Shelby outside. *Gut!* Going around the house, she opened the bulkhead doors. She checked the spot in the cellar where she wanted to set the supers before hurrying up the kitchen stairs to stuff the sheet into the crack beneath the door. There mustn't be any chance of bees sneaking into the house.

With care, she carried the supers to the pair of two-by-fours that would allow for air circulation into the bottom of the hive. She brought the other two and set them beside the first set. She shut the bulkhead doors and switched on the lantern to spread light across the stone floor.

"Can I watch while you put the queen in?" Daniel asked from the top of the kitchen stairs. He stepped onto the first step without waiting for her answer.

"There's not much to see, but come ahead. Make sure you close the door and stuff that fabric under it."

Daniel did as she requested.

"There's a flashlight on the shelf up there," Hannah called. "You'd better use it so you don't fall and break your neck."

"I appreciate you worrying about me taking a tumble. I'm glad you're not still angry with me."

"If I was, all I needed to do was let you help me move the bees."

He chuckled. "You've got plenty of bees down here. You aren't going to sic them on me, are you?"

Hoping she wasn't being a fool, she put her hand on his arm. "The past is the past, Daniel. Didn't you say that the day Shelby arrived?" She stood straighter, though she was more than six inches shorter than he was. "If you've changed your mind and want to linger in the past, fine. Just don't expect me to."

He opened his mouth to retort, but closed it.

Did he want to avoid an argument, or was he unwilling to admit he agreed with her?

Knowing she couldn't keep the queen from her anxious hive, Hannah picked up the small plastic container. She set the lantern on a nearby shelf and adjusted it so the light shone on the pair of supers she'd set on top of the screen spanning the two by fours. As she stepped closer, she could hear the rapid buzzing from the uneasy bees. She lifted one corner of the uppermost super's lid and slipped the end of the plastic container under it.

She tapped the queen and other bees out and watched them crawl among the combs lashed to the frames with rubber bands. As she lowered the lid, she saw bees moving toward their queen. Nothing would calm them more than her presence.

"Will you hand me the piece of mesh over there?" Hannah asked.

"What is it?" Daniel asked as he handed it to her.

"A queen excluder." She set the simple plastic mesh on top of the supers. "It has holes worker bees can pass through, but not the queen who's larger. The queen excluder will insure she doesn't fly off while the hive is getting accustomed to their new home."

Making sure the mesh was set squarely on the box, she picked up the other supers and set them on the first ones. She took care to avoid squashing bees. Finally she looked around the cellar.

"What do you need?" Daniel asked.

"That piece of plywood. It goes on top of the supers." She pointed to the wood leaning against the shelves holding the last of the canned peaches she'd put up last summer.

They maneuvered it on the hive. On each side, it was about an inch wider than the boxes. He moved aside and watched when she took a ragged quilt from the shelf. Swinging it over the hive, she watched the quilt puddle on the floor in every direction, darkening the hive and offering no escape for the bees. However, air could sift through the fabric and reach the combs, so the bees didn't suffocate.

"And that's that," she said, walking around the hive and adjusting the quilt on each side before she set bricks on it to keep the fabric from shifting. "We'll leave them in the dark. When they come out, they'll have no idea they're not much more than a stone's throw from their old hive." She smiled. "It'll help that you're taking out the rotten board."

"I had no idea how to take care of bees. I'm glad I contacted you."

She pulled off her gloves and yanked the tabs on her protective shirt. Shrugging it off, she folded it over her arm after making sure no bees clung to it. "And I'm glad, too, that we've saved the bees."

"How long will they be here?"

"About a week or so. Maybe two. It has to be long enough for them to forget where they were before. The cold helps because they're less active, and the rain we've been having will wash away the scent trails quickly. By the time I move this hive beside my others, warmer weather should be here and the first flowers blooming. The bees can then do what they do best, gathering nectar and spreading pollen and making honey."

"I'll be glad to help you when you're ready to move them outside, if you need help."

"I appreciate that." And she did, which surprised her. The past few days hadn't been easy, but they also hadn't been the end of the world. Daniel had shown he could be a *gut* friend by helping her with Shelby. He'd revealed he did have a heart by how gently he treated her great-grandmother. "Let's get out of here ourselves."

She walked to the cupboard where she kept her equipment and beekeeper's clothing. Putting away each piece, she made sure the kerchief she wore over her hair was in place. She turned around and gasped when she discovered Daniel standing right behind her.

He grasped her chin and tilted it so the lantern's light played across her left cheek. "What happened to you?"

How could she have forgotten the mark on her face? *Help me, Lord*, she prayed. *I can't tell the whole truth, because I don't know what will happen to us then. Help me find the right words. I have to protect my family. They're all I have.*

"Just an accident," she replied, hoping he'd leave it at that.

He didn't. "What type of accident?"

"I was down at the bridge earlier. I wanted to check on the hive once more before I moved them. It was raining, and the grass was wet." She stepped away from him. "You can guess what happened next."

Would he accept her story that was true but didn't include the part about her great-grandmother losing her temper? She held her breath.

Puzzlement dimmed his dark eyes, and she knew he was trying to believe her. When he motioned for her to lead the way up the stairs to the kitchen, she felt relief and regret. She wished she could depend on someone else, most especially Daniel, but how could she when the one time she'd dared to trust him, he'd left her as her *daed* had?

Chapter Seven

"*Gute mariye*, my girls." *Grossmammi* Ella came into the kitchen with a broad smile at dawn early the next week.

"Good morning." Hannah flashed a smile over her shoulder. She stood by the stove frying eggs. She was relieved to hear her great-grandmother's happy tone. Though the elderly woman's mood could change in a split second, when *Grossmammi* Ella's voice was filled with joy, the day usually went well.

In the distance, Hannah could hear the equipment used by Daniel's crew on the Hunter's Mill Creek Bridge. They had begun tearing off the rotten boards the day after Hannah moved the bees. Behind the concrete barriers, piles of debris had been swelling, but she'd noticed this morning when she raised the shade on her bedroom window that the wood was being loaded in a beat-up truck to be carted away. Faint laughter had reached the house as the men worked together.

Smelling the eggs starting to scorch, she flipped them. At the same time, her great-grandmother announced, "I have something here."

"What is it?" She scraped at a spot where the eggs had stuck to the pan.

"It's for the *boppli*."

Hannah took the cast iron pan off the stove so she could give the older woman her complete attention. She wiped her hands on her apron to make sure there was no grease on them and then took the toy held out to her. *Grossmammi* Ella had knit its body and head before stuffing it with rags. Bright yellow and black, she guessed it was meant to be a honeybee. The old woman must have made it during the quiet times she spent in her bedroom each afternoon.

Until that moment, Hannah had wondered if her great-grandmother would accept Shelby as a member of their family. Doing that meant *Grossmammi* Ella had to admit her grandson had left the toddler behind as he had Hannah. Or perhaps her great-grandmother simply wanted to make a lonely *kind* happy.

"Don't you want to give it to Shelby?" Hannah asked.

"Ja." Walking with care to where the little girl sat in her high chair, *Grossmammi* Ella placed

the knit toy on the edge of the tray. She wiggled it, catching Shelby's attention. "See, my friend, little one?"

Shelby poked one finger at the toy. When the elderly woman slid it across the high chair tray, the *kind* laughed.

Hannah was astonished when the little girl pursed her lips and made a whirring sound by blowing through them. The toddler was copying the noise Hannah had made the previous evening while reading her a picture book about a busy bee and its attempt to find a flower. Hannah hadn't been certain the *kind* had understood the story, but realized Shelby had connected the sound with the picture of a bee in the book.

What else did the toddler understand? Hannah hoped the therapists the *doktorfraa* was sending would be able to help her answer the question. And wouldn't Daniel be amazed when she told him what Shelby had done!

Hannah stared at her wooden spoon which was halfway between the pan and the plate she used for serving the eggs. She hadn't expected *that* thought. Was Daniel wheedling his way into her life—into their lives—again? The idea should have annoyed her, but all she could think of was how pleased he'd be when she told him about Shelby comprehending the story.

Things had changed—again—between her

and Daniel. They hadn't been friends before, because she'd fallen so hard and fast for him. Was what they shared now friendship? A friendship could make their bargain more comfortable for them instead of being lit by the white-hot intensity of the infatuation she'd had. She wondered if any young man could have lived up to the fantasy she'd built. Especially one like Daniel who'd made no promises other than they'd have fun together.

"Sounds like she's saying buzz-buzz-buzz," said *Grossmammi* Ella, pulling Hannah from her surprising thoughts.

"Buzz-buzz would be a *gut* name," Hannah said with a smile. "*Danki, Grossmammi* Ella, for making her a special gift."

"A *boppli* needs toys. Soft toys to hug." Her great-grandmother sounded gruff, and Hannah guessed she was trying to hide her satisfaction at how thrilled Shelby was with her gift. "When will breakfast be ready?"

"Right away."

The rest of the morning passed as pleasantly as breakfast. Shelby continued playing with the stuffed bee much to *Grossmammi* Ella's delight. That gave Hannah time to take care of the animals, including the bees in the cellar, and to do her other chores. The two in the living room made up games together, the elderly woman in her favorite chair and the *kind* leaning against her knee as she made the bee "fly." Laughter filled the house that had been somber for too long.

During the midday meal, *Grossmammi* Ella spoke about the flowers she wanted to plant by the front steps once the weather was warm. Hannah listened while making a mental list of the annuals she'd buy for her great-grandmother at one of the greenhouses in Paradise Springs.

When the elderly woman retreated to her bedroom, Hannah tried to keep Shelby quiet. The little girl refused to nap and fussed with her sore mouth. One tooth had popped through over the weekend, but another was already giving her misery. *Grossmammi* Ella needed to rest, so Hannah put some honey on Shelby's sore gum and tried to rock her to sleep. The little girl refused to settle and continued to cry.

Hannah felt weak tears flood her eyes when she heard footfalls on the porch just as Shelby was falling asleep. The *kind* routed awake. Rising, Hannah opened the door.

Daniel stood there, his clothes dirty with the road dust ingrained in the boards on the old bridge. Her heart jumped, astonishing her. Her traitorous heart had done that in the past, but it shouldn't now. She knew better.

"I can't stay long." His lowered voice resonated through the house like the rumble of distant traffic. Taking off his straw hat, he held it in front of him. "I wanted—" He paused as Shelby offered her new toy to him. "What do you have there, *liebling*?"

Shelby made the buzzing sound before giggling with excitement.

"She's trying to tell you," Hannah said, "the bee's name is Buzz-buzz." She quickly explained how Shelby had connected the stuffed toy with the story Hannah had read to her and the sounds she'd made for the little girl. "*Grossmammi* Ella made it for her."

When Daniel took the toy and examined it, Shelby watched him. He handed it to her, and she pretended to make it fly.

He laughed. "That's right." He winked at Hannah. "Though I doubt most bees fly upside down, do they?"

"Toy ones do." She set the little girl on the sofa. "What do you want, Daniel?"

"A couple of things. First, I hope the noise from the bridge hasn't been a bother."

"No, it's been fine. It won't go on too long, will it?"

"We need to be done in under six weeks." He turned his hat around and around by the brim, startling her because she hadn't expected him to be nervous. "The other thing I wanted to say was you should come to the supper at the Paradise

Springs Fire Department tonight. We're raising money for new equipment and hoping for a big turnout. Will you come?"

"It may be too late in the day for my great-grandmother and Shelby."

He shook his head. "Nope. The supper starts at six, and it's for a *gut* cause. In addition, it would do you *gut*, Hannah, to get out and spend the evening beyond these four walls."

Hannah hesitated. For the past couple of years, she hadn't taken her great-grandmother many places because *Grossmammi* Ella always had an excuse at the last minute not to go. It was easier to stay home. But this supper was different. Many of the volunteer firefighters in Paradise Springs were plain, and the Amish community supported the volunteers who protected their homes and other buildings. She'd heard people talking about the supper after the church service on Sunday, so there would be familiar faces there. And Daniel was right. It was for a *gut* cause.

"All I can say is maybe," she replied.

"Anything I can say or do to turn that maybe into a *ja*?" His eyes twinkled.

Again her heart did a little dance. As it had when he used to flirt with her. She'd forgotten how *gut* that felt.

"Maybe," she replied.

He grinned. "Is maybe all you can say?"

"Maybe."

Starting to laugh, he clapped his hand over his mouth so he didn't wake her great-grandmother. He winked again and ruffled Shelby's hair. "Then *maybe*, I'll see you tonight."

His easy smile sent warmth spiraling through her, even after he was gone. It should have been enough to convince her to stay away from the firehouse tonight, but she wanted to go. She couldn't remember the last time she'd gone anywhere but on errands or to attend church.

It was time to change that.

As Hannah had expected, when she suggested attending the fund-raising supper, her great-grandmother was reluctant to go. Hannah's insistence they support the firefighters convinced *Grossmammi* Ella.

Or so Hannah thought. She realized how mistaken she was when, after she'd hitched up the buggy horse, she came into the house and discovered her great-grandmother standing in the front room and watching Shelby play.

"It looks like Hannah is taking to the bee, ain't so, Saloma?" the old woman asked.

Hannah flinched. Her great-grandmother was lost in time again. The changes came without warning. *Grossmammi* Ella thought Hannah was her granddaughter-in-law and Shelby was Hannah. Last year, Hannah had paid no attention to these misconceptions, telling herself everyone mixed up names once in a while. She couldn't ignore them any longer. It was part of the sickness stealing *Grossmammi* Ella's mind.

After taking her great-grandmother to a specialist, Hannah knew how each step of the disease would progress. She also knew there was little that could halt it. The *doktor* had written a prescription for a medicine to slow the inevitable, but *Grossmammi* Ella refused to take it after the pills made her sick and dizzy.

Hannah hadn't insisted. Not after her great-grandmother in a lucid moment had said if her days on earth were numbered, she preferred not to spend them weak and nauseated. Unable to argue with that, Hannah had taken her great-grandmother to Dr. Montgomery for regular checkups. The *doktorfraa* accepted the elderly woman's determination to live her life on her terms.

"She loves it," Hannah replied to her great-grandmother's question about the stuffed toy. As long as *Grossmammi* Ella didn't do anything to hurt herself or someone else, Hannah let her keep her illusions. "She'll enjoy it while we're at the supper at the fire station."

"You're letting her take it with her?"

"Ja."

"You spoil that *kind*." The sharp edge had returned to the old woman's voice. Her abrupt mood swings were impossible to anticipate.

"*Bopplin* should be spoiled." Hannah kept her voice light. "It makes them happy, and it makes us happy, too."

Her great-grandmother sniffed once at Hannah's reply and a second time while taking her cane. "Mark my words, Saloma. You're spoiling that *kind*, and who knows how she'll turn out?"

"We'll have to wait and see what the future brings, ain't so?"

Relief flooded Hannah when *Grossmammi* Ella didn't reply as they walked out to the buggy. Though it made driving difficult, Hannah made sure the toddler was sitting to her right instead of between her and her great-grandmother. There was the possibility the elderly woman would become upset and strike out at the nearest person. Hannah didn't want Shelby to be the target.

She touched her cheek where the bruise had almost faded. The *doktorfraa*'s words haunted her: "If your great-grandmother gets to the point where she's a danger to herself and others, we'll have to discuss the best options for her and for you, Hannah. I know you want to keep her living with you, but you can't put both of you in peril."

Now three of them lived in the house, and

Daniel was there often. She hoped *Grossmammi* Ella wouldn't get worse anytime soon.

The fire station was bright with electric lights and the flashers on the fire engines when Hannah drove the buggy into the parking lot between it and the post office. *Kinder* gathered around the trucks and firemen, calling out questions and examining the firefighting tools the volunteers held. No *kind* was allowed near the axes, but they didn't seem to mind. They were having too much fun trying on helmets and sitting behind the wheel while a fireman activated the siren.

"You came!" Daniel's voice reached her as she opened the buggy's door.

Where was he?

He grinned as he edged out of the darkness, and her breath caught. His black hair shone with blue fire beneath the powerful electric lights. Crinkled with laughter, his eyes snapped with the same blue sparks. Though dozens of voices were raised in conversation in every direction, her ears had picked out his as if it were the only one.

Before she could answer, Shelby started babbling and holding out her short arms to him. He picked up the toddler as he said, "*Komm* with me. I'll show you around."

Hannah assisted her great-grandmother from the buggy and followed him toward the firehouse. He stopped again and again to point out something to Shelby who chewed on her stuffed toy to ease her sore gums. When he reached the building, he waited for her and *Grossmammi* Ella to catch up.

She blinked when they entered the large space where the fire trucks were usually parked. Tables had been arranged in rows with baskets of rolls placed every three or four chairs. The aroma of tomato sauce and taco spices drifted from where the buffet tables were. It was a haystack dinner, and her stomach growled in eager expectancy of the flavors of beef, rice, green peppers and cheese as well as onions, olives and salsa. Everything would be piled together on their plates, each flavor enhancing the others.

Daniel walked to where a woman with graying hair was setting out stacks of cups. She smiled.

"*Grossmammi* Ella, Hannah, Shelby," he said, nodding in his head toward each of them as he spoke their names, "this is my *mamm*, Wanda Stoltzfus. *Mamm*, you remember these lovely Lambright ladies I've told you about."

Hannah appreciated Daniel introducing them to his *mamm* just in case *Grossmammi* Ella had met Wanda before and failed to remember her. There was a definite resemblance between Daniel and his *mamm*. Something about the shape of their faces and their easy smiles.

After greeting them, Wanda said, "It's so *gut* to see you again, *Grossmammi* Ella. Not that you probably remember me. It's been more than twenty years since the last time we've done more than wave while driving past each other along the road."

"I remember your husband," the older woman said.

"I'm not surprised. Paul knew everyone from the Chester County line to Harrisburg."

Grossmammi Ella gasped. "Knew? Your husband is dead?"

Hannah put her hands on her great-grandmother's arms and steered her to a nearby chair. The blunt questions had dimmed Wanda's bright eyes. Wanting to tell Daniel's *mamm* that *Grossmammi* Ella hadn't meant to say anything hurtful, Hannah stayed silent. She couldn't embarrass her great-grandmother. She handed the old woman a roll from the nearest basket.

"I need butter," her great-grandmother said.

"I'll get some. Stay here."

Hannah went to get several pats of butter from a serving table. Each person she passed smiled and welcomed her to the haystack dinner. She wondered if the prodigal son had felt like she did. Everyone acted as if they'd missed her. People she'd never met greeted her like a long-lost friend.

She took butter to *Grossmammi* Ella and

helped her put it on the roll. With the old woman occupied with eating, Hannah's eyes searched the room for Wanda Stoltzfus and discovered her stacking paper napkins next to the cups.

Going to Daniel's *mamm*, Hannah said, "Wanda, I'm so sorry. *Grossmammi* Ella didn't mean—"

"I know." She put a gentle hand on Hannah's arm. "Sometimes our elders forget matters, big and small. I'd like to think it's because the *gut* Lord wants to ease their burden of carrying so many memories, letting them know He forgives past wrongs and has rejoiced with them on past joys. He lightens their hearts, making them ready to soar when their time comes to go home to Him."

Hannah blinked on sudden, scalding tears. In her isolation, she'd forgotten the comfort a kind word could bring. Wanda's words reached deep within her and loosened the thick web of futility growing there, capturing every hurt *Grossmammi* Ella didn't intend to inflict. Her great-grandmother had been a loving woman... until the past couple of years. Turning away, she hid her tears.

"If you're looking for your little girl," Wanda went on, "Daniel is showing her the fire trucks outside. Go ahead. I'll keep an eye on your great-grandmother." She held up one finger. "Just a moment." Walking over to the desserts table, she picked up a handful of cookies and brought them to Hannah. "Why don't you take these with you? There has never been a *kind* who doesn't love my cookies." She chuckled. "Or one of my grown-up sons either."

"I wish giving her cookies would convince Shelby to like me more."

Wanda clasped Hannah's shoulder. "Do you think it's because you look so much like your *daed*?"

Shock froze her. She could barely remember what her *daed* looked like and had come to assume he resembled his *grossmammi*. "I do?"

"*Ja*. Shelby can see that, too. Do you think it's possible she's wary of you because you remind her of your *daed*, and she's afraid you'll abandon her as he did?"

She stared at Wanda in astonishment. "Really?"

"I may be way off base, but it's the only explanation that makes sense to me. You treat her with love."

"*Grossmammi* Ella tells me I spoil her."

"If loving a *kind* is spoiling her, then I agree with your great-grandmother." Wanda waved her away. "Go and spend time with the other young people. Enjoy your evening out, Hannah."

A smile tilted her lips. "I will." Without another word, she headed in the direction Wanda had indicated.

When she stepped outside, Daniel motioned for her to come over to where he had Shelby sitting on his shoulders while he spoke with several men. He introduced Hannah to the firefighters gathered there. She wished his saucy expression each time he looked at her didn't cause the butterflies inside her to take flight. Hadn't she learned her lesson? Daniel flirted with every woman, whether she was as young as Shelby or as elderly as *Grossmammi* Ella. There was, she told herself, nothing special in his grin for her.

But maybe, for this evening, she'd let the past stay in the past and enjoy herself as Wanda had suggested. She hoped she hadn't forgotten how.

Daniel felt his heart trying to do somersaults in his chest when he stood with the Lambrights in a dusky corner at the end of the evening. Until he'd seen her in the parking lot, he doubted Hannah would come tonight. She'd shut herself off from the rest of the community for two years. He admitted to himself he was relieved to know it hadn't been for three years. Then he would have blamed himself for her withdrawal. He knew his actions hadn't helped, but he guessed her great-grandmother's strange ways kept her from spending time with the rest of the residents of Paradise Springs.

Beside him, *Grossmammi* Ella was struggling to get into her coat. He helped her, but his gaze refused to leave Hannah. The bruise had faded from her face, leaving her cheek soft and pink once more. His fingers quivered at the thought of brushing them against her skin or through the rich honey of her hair.

He couldn't look away as she buttoned Shelby's coat. Did Hannah think he didn't see how she glanced at her great-grandmother to check *Grossmammi* Ella's coat was closed, too?

He'd noticed *Mamm* watching how Hannah had spent most of the meal overseeing her great-grandmother as well as the toddler. He wasn't surprised. His *mamm* cared about every member of their community almost as much as she did her *kinder*. That was why she was eager to see each of her *kinder* settled in a happy marriage. He had no doubts about her *gut* intentions, and he guessed, after tonight, she'd have several dozen questions about Hannah and her little family.

"*Danki* for asking us to attend," Hannah said as she stood and held Shelby's hand.

"Insisting, you mean." He gave her a cockeyed grin, hoping she'd respond to his teasing.

He was rewarded when she chuckled. When they were walking out together, he hadn't had to resort to jesting in order to banish her serious expression. Her eyes had brightened like twin lamps the moment her gaze met his, and her lips had offered a sweet smile. So much trust she'd invested in him. Too much for the young man he'd been.

"Everyone has been nice," she said. "I don't know why I'm surprised. Whenever I bring honey to Amos's shop, everyone says hello."

"The people of Paradise Springs are close-knit. It may be because we live so close to the highway and the *Englisch* world. That makes us appreciate each other."

"But you have *Englischers* among you." She looked across the room to where several families, who were not plain, were chatting with the Amish and Mennonite families sharing their tables.

"The fire department welcomes everyone who wants to protect Paradise Springs. Nobody cares if you're plain or not. Everyone is determined to keep a fire from taking a neighbor's house or barn. Sharing a common goal gives us common ground to build friendships upon." He grinned. "Sort of like you and me. Our goals might not have been in common, but they intersected."

She scooped up Shelby who was trying to tug away and join other youngsters running around the empty tables. "*Danki* again for inviting us,

Daniel. *Grossmammi* Ella has talked so much she's hoarse, and I don't think Shelby's feet touched the floor all night."

"She's a friendly tyke."

"*Ja*, though she's leery of certain people."

"You mean you."

"Your *mamm* thinks it's because she sees too much of our *daed* in me."

His brows shot up. "I never thought of that."

"Me neither." She bid him good-night and walked with her great-grandmother and the toddler to their buggy.

He stood in the doorway, watching as they drove away. When he went into the firehouse, it seemed as if the lights were a bit duller and the conversation subdued. He helped clean up before he brought his buggy around so his *mamm* could get in.

The road leading through the village and toward their farm was deserted. He waited for *Mamm* to mention Hannah and her family, but she seemed lost in thought. He listened to Taffy's iron shoes on the road, the creak of the buggy wheels and the fine mist falling around them.

As the buggy rolled to a stop by the house, he said, "Here we are."

"*Ja*. Here we are." She half turned on the seat to look at him, her face in a silhouette against the soft glow from the kitchen windows. "After seeing you and Hannah tonight, I do want you to recall, my son, it was you who decided you didn't want to continue walking out with her." There was no censure in her voice.

"I know. I was young and foolish then."

"You aren't so young. Are you still as foolish?"

He grinned and shook his head. "I'd like to say no, but how many times have you told us that changing the past is impossible? That we must ask for forgiveness for our mistakes and move forward, making sure we never choose poorly again."

She got out of the buggy. "Remember a mistake is no longer a mistake if you remedy it in time."

"I'm not sure I can do that."

"Because you don't want to?"

"No, because the time to correct it is long past."

She regarded him for a long time, and he fought not to squirm as if he were a *kind* again. "I hope you're wrong, Daniel."

He watched as she went into the cozy *dawdi haus*. When the door closed behind her, he murmured to himself and the night and God, "I hope I am, too."

Chapter Eight

Two days after the haystack dinner at the firehouse, Hannah heard a car coming along the road before she saw it through the steady rain. A blue SUV slowed at the junction leading to the covered bridge, then began inching toward the house.

She glanced at the clock on the mantel. It was almost ten o'clock. The physical therapist's message, left on the neighbors' answering machine, was to expect her around ten this morning.

The car pulled into the driveway and parked. The driver's door opened, and a bright yellow umbrella appeared. Snapping open, it rose along with the woman emerging from the car. Hooking a large purse over her arm, she slammed the door closed and rushed toward the house, skirting the large puddles marking every depression in the yard.

Hannah threw open the door as the *Englischer* climbed the porch steps. "*Komm* in!"

"Don't mind if I do." The woman shook her umbrella and sprayed water across the porch before she closed it. "Hi, I'm Audrey Powell. Are you Hannah?"

"*Ja.*"

Audrey Powell was about as old as Hannah's *mamm* would have been, but she had a cheeky smile and was as spry as a teenager. Gray streaked the brown hair she wore in a ponytail. Her t-shirt had a big-eyed cat on the front, and her sneakers had pink-and-blue laces wound together and tied in big bows.

Those bows fascinated Shelby who couldn't take her eyes off them. Pushing herself to her feet, she waddled to Audrey and dropped to the floor in front of the sneakers. She reached out to touch the bright bows.

"Hello, Shelby," said Audrey, squatting in front of the little girl. She waved Hannah back, clearly wanting to see how the *kind* reacted to her.

Shelby made some of the sounds she used instead of words, but her gaze remained focused on the bows.

"Do you like my shoes, Shelby?" the physical therapist asked before looking up at Hannah. "Does she understand English?"

Hannah nodded. "She's been living with my

daed—my father, and, as far as we can figure out, she's used to *Englisch*. I don't think she understands much *Deitsch*."

"That's good, because my *Deitsch* is pretty basic." She gave Hannah a reassuring smile. "I've worked with plain folk before, so I understand your children speak *Deitsch* until they begin school. I also know the Amish don't attend public schools where ongoing therapy is provided for any child requiring it. However, where she'll go to school won't make a difference in evaluating Shelby and developing an IEP for her. An Individualized Education Program." She chuckled. "We get used to talking in acronyms, so stop me whenever I use one you don't understand."

"Are you a *doktorfraa*?" demanded *Grossmammi* Ella as she walked into the room, her cane banging against the floor to emphasize her vexation at finding a stranger in her house. That she used the cane revealed she didn't want the *Englischer* to see any weakness in her.

"No, ma'am," Audrey said. "I'm a physical therapist. Dr. Montgomery asked me to come here to work with Shelby."

Hannah introduced the two women. She wished she'd had time to warn the therapist about her great-grandmother's sudden shifts in mood.

Urging the elderly woman to use a chair by the stove where she'd stay warm on the damp day, Hannah wasn't surprised when her great-grandmother asked another question as she sat, "You can help our Shelby?"

"I can make sure she gets the right help so she can become all you hope her to be." Audrey didn't seem bothered by the question.

Grossmammi Ella nodded and folded her hands on her lap. "Go ahead."

Audrey arched her brows at Hannah who struggled not to smile at her great-grandmother's regal edict.

"Where do you want to work with Shelby?" Hannah asked.

"Here on the rug will be fine." She grinned. "I find sessions go best when I'm on the children's level." Sitting cross-legged on the floor, she motioned for Hannah to join her and Shelby.

Kneeling next to the therapist, Hannah held her breath. Would Shelby cooperate with whatever Audrey had planned? Would *Grossmammi* Ella refrain from interrupting? She took a steadying breath to calm herself and sent up a prayer for serenity.

"Shelby," Audrey said with a smile, "let's play a game."

The toddler stood, ran across the room and got the knitted honeybee she'd dropped when the therapist had arrived. She held it out to Audrey.

"How cute!" the therapist gushed, earning a

wide smile from Shelby and one almost as big from *Grossmammi* Ella.

"Its name is Buzz-buzz," Hannah said.

"Did Shelby give the toy that name?"

"Not exactly." She explained how Shelby had made a buzzing sound when she first saw the toy. "But she must like the name because she responds when we ask where Buzz-buzz is."

"How does she respond?"

"She points to it or goes and gets it."

Audrey smiled. "That's excellent. Some toddlers who don't have Shelby's challenges aren't able to follow even simple instructions at this age." Looking at the *kind*, she asked, "Shelby, can I hold Buzz-buzz?"

The little girl hesitated, then handed the toy to Audrey, who cooed over it. Shelby laughed, and when Audrey held out the toy, she took it and hugged it hard as she pursed her lips, making the buzzing sound.

"What other toys does she like to play with?" the therapist asked.

Before Hannah could reply, a knock came on the door. It opened, and Daniel walked in. He shrugged off his wet coat and hung it by the door. Doing so revealed the strong muscles barely hidden beneath his plain shirt and black suspenders. For a moment, as she watched his smooth motions, she seemed to have forgotten how to breathe.

"Where's my big girl?" he asked with a smile.

"Da-da!" called Shelby, waving her arms at him.

Hannah froze and saw Daniel do the same, shock on his face. Why was Shelby calling out to Daniel as if he were her *daed*? The answer came when Shelby spoke again.

"Da-dan," she called. She was trying to say Daniel rather than the *Englisch* word *daddy*. "Da-dan!" Impatience heightened her voice.

Daniel squatted beside Shelby. "How are you doing, *liebling*?" He took the knit toy and tickled her with it.

Audrey looked from him to Hannah. "I'm confused. Aren't you, Hannah, Shelby's sister?"

"I am," Hannah said.

At the same time, Daniel replied, "I'm Daniel Stoltzfus."

"But she called you *da-da*," Audrey said, bafflement threading her brow.

Hannah said, "No, she was trying to say Daniel."

Understanding crossed the therapist's face, and her smile returned. "You understand the sounds she makes better than I do. Does she use other words you recognize?"

Hannah shook her head. "She hasn't used *Da-dan* before today."

"Does she have a name for you?"

Hoping her face wasn't bright red, for heat soared through her like a wildfire, she said, "Not yet."

"That will come, I'm sure. Will Shelby be getting speech therapy, too?"

"*Ja*. Dr. Montgomery said she was contacting someone to help Shelby."

"Probably Todd Howland. You'll like him, and Shelby will, too. He's great with kids. Most likely, you'll be hearing from Keely Mattera, too. She's the occupational therapist, and the three of us work as a team with young children."

Audrey called Shelby's name and, when the little girl looked up, asked her to touch her nose as Audrey was. The toddler followed along with what she saw as a game. When the therapist took Shelby by the hand, they went to the stairs in the front hall and practiced stepping up and down off the lowest one. Shelby did, but on her hands and knees. When the therapist lifted her to her feet and urged her to try again, the *kind*'s lower lip began to tremble in a pout.

"Hannah, will you try to convince her?" Audrey asked.

Knowing it was unlikely the toddler would heed anything she said or did, Hannah stepped forward. Shelby let out a frustrated howl and sat on the step.

"Can I try?" Daniel asked.

Audrey glanced at Hannah, who nodded. If Shelby would cooperate with Daniel, they couldn't leave him out of the sessions. Even knowing that didn't make it easy for her to move aside.

"Let's go, Shelby," he said, copying Audrey's motions. "It's fun, ain't so?"

The little girl giggled and gave him a big grin before going up and down with him. When Audrey asked her to go up and down two steps, Shelby seemed eager to prove she could.

Hannah choked back her dismay. Shelby preferred anyone else to her sister. Was Wanda right? Was Shelby pushing Hannah away because of the resemblance to their *daed*? It seemed weird the toddler would avoid the one person connected to her and her parents.

Or…? Hannah didn't want to let the thought form in her head. *Daed* had been a gentle man, but he'd been changed by his wife's death. She'd assumed he was the same loving person he'd been with her at Shelby's age. Maybe he wasn't.

She looked away from where Daniel and Shelby were traversing three steps at a time. Her distress at her unwanted thoughts vanished when she saw the chair where *Grossmammi* Ella had been sitting was empty. Where had she gone?

Dread sank through her. Wandering was another aspect of her great-grandmother's disease. How was Hannah going to watch both her and Shelby's sessions at once?

For the first time, she thought of Daniel's offer of having Shelby live with his family. His *mamm* was kind and capable, having already raised nine *kinder*. Shelby would have a *gut* home where Hannah could visit her, and *Grossmammi* Ella would be easier to keep track of when she had all of Hannah's attention. And Daniel wouldn't be coming to her house every day, looking so easy on the eyes and being so nice her resolve to avoid him was melting away.

Letting him take Shelby would be the smart thing to do, but Hannah knew she'd never say the words and end up depending on him. Not again.

"I'll be right back," she said, rushing from the front hall.

Daniel stared after Hannah in disbelief. She was leaving right in the middle of Shelby's therapy?

Audrey continued watching the toddler on the stairs, but Daniel saw her glance in the direction Hannah had gone. Torn between going after Hannah and helping Shelby, he heard Hannah call out her great-grandmother's name just before the back door slammed shut.

Suddenly, like a clap of thunder, he realized what was going on. The chair where the old woman had been sitting was empty. Where was *Grossmammi* Ella? He'd been so focused on Shelby he hadn't noticed the elderly woman leaving.

When Audrey led Shelby into the living room, the therapist sat on the floor and began to stack blocks, motioning for Shelby to do the same.

"Will you be helping with Shelby's therapy?" Audrey asked into the silence, and Daniel guessed, though she kept her expression neutral, she was as shocked by Hannah's sudden disappearance as he'd been.

"*Ja.* At least, I hope so. Shelby likes when I play with her, and a lot of what you're doing looks like a game."

The physical therapist smiled. "We try to make it feel like that for little ones, so they're more willing to participate. I wish we could find a way to make it fun for adults, too, but they see right through our wiles."

He tried to concentrate on what the therapist was doing so he could repeat the exercises with the toddler, but he couldn't halt himself from glancing again and again toward the kitchen. When the back door opened, he buried his impulse to jump up and help Hannah guide her great-grandmother in.

Shelby shouted with excitement when her tower of blocks tumbled, but Hannah said nothing as her great-grandmother shuffled into her bedroom. When the door closed behind *Grossmammi* Ella, a long sigh drifted from Hannah. She walked toward them.

"I'm sorry I had to leave. Everything's fine," Hannah said with a strained laugh. "I wanted to make sure my great-grandmother had a warm coat while she was outside. But she decided to come in, so all's well."

A dozen questions demanded answers, but Daniel didn't ask a single one. Audrey might believe Hannah's excuse. He didn't. Her great-grandmother shouldn't have been out in the rain in the first place.

After the therapist showed Hannah the exercise she was doing with Shelby and the blocks, Audrey stood and smiled. "That's enough for today. I don't want to tire her out on our first day. I'll fill out my portion of the paperwork for her IEP. When Keely and Todd have done their sections, we'll submit it for review. Once it's complete, we'll put together a schedule that works for you and Shelby. We don't want to overwhelm you. We hope this little sweetheart will continue to cooperate with the exercises we give her."

"Danki," Hannah said. "If you need anything, let me know."

"I will. Leaving a message on your neighbor's phone is okay?"

"Ja. They'll let me know, and I'll contact you."

Slinging her bag over her shoulder, the therapist bid them and Shelby goodbye. The door closed behind her, and Daniel waited until the sound of her footsteps vanished off the porch.

"Is your great-grandmother all right?" he asked.

Hannah nodded, but she didn't meet his worried gaze. Did she think she could hide her agitation from him? Again he discovered he'd misjudged her reaction when she sat on the sofa and clasped her hands.

"Are *you* all right?" he asked as he sat beside her.

"A bit overwhelmed." She raised her eyes, and he saw she was being honest. "I'm not sure how I'm going to help Shelby with her exercises when she wants nothing to do with me."

"You'll figure out something. You always do. I admire that about you, Hannah. You don't hesitate to run in where angels fear to tread."

"Something that's foolish to do."

"Not foolish. Caring and courageous."

Astonishment softened her face, and he wondered when someone had last offered her a compliment. The Amish weren't supposed to praise one another, but it happened far more often than anyone was willing to admit. Had anyone told Hannah how pretty she was since he had...three years ago? Had anyone told her how *wunderbaar* she was since he had...three years ago? Had anyone told her how special she was? He hadn't, not even three years ago. He'd accepted the gift of her loving heart though he wasn't willing to offer his in return.

"I'm doing what I need to do," she said, lowering her eyes again.

His hand was cupping her chin, bringing her gaze to his, before he had a chance to think. "I know, but you're special, Hannah."

"You'd do the same as I am."

"I'd like to think I would, but I'm not so sure. I hope I don't have to find out."

"I hope you don't either." She shifted her head from his grip. "You're right."

"Me? Right? I never thought I'd hear Hannah Lambright say that."

Her eyes began to shine with mischief, something he'd seen too seldom since he'd found her little sister on the porch. "I'd have admitted you were right before if you'd ever been right."

He laughed, but the sound faded when Shelby walked over to them, carrying Buzz-buzz. The little girl glanced from her sister to him as if trying to figure something out. Without a word, she held up the stuffed bee. Not to him, but to Hannah. She looked at her older sister and grinned.

Tears glistened in Hannah's eyes, and Daniel found himself smiling so broadly it hurt. For the first time, the little girl was reaching out to Hannah.

Hannah took the toy and rubbed it against her cheek before doing the same to Shelby's. The little girl giggled.

"Try playing peekaboo with her," he suggested.

"That's your game."

He understood what she didn't say. Hannah wanted to have something special only she and her little sister shared. When the *kind* took the knitted toy, she held it to her face before dropping it on Hannah's apron. Shelby ran across the room to the bookshelf. Plucking a book off it, she rushed back to the sofa and set it beside the toy on Hannah's knees.

Hannah drew in a quick breath.

"What's wrong?" he asked.

"Nothing's wrong." She picked up the book and smiled at the little girl, tears of joy hanging on her lashes. "It's the book I've been reading to her. The one about bees. Would you like me to read it to you, Shelby?"

The *kind* nodded so hard her golden hair bounced around her. When she opened her arms and raised them toward Hannah, Daniel felt his own eyes sting with unexpected tears. He'd prayed for this moment when Shelby would realize the person who cared most about her in the whole world was her sister.

As Hannah lifted the toddler onto her lap and opened the book while Shelby cuddled Buzz-buzz, he stood and went to the door. He said goodbye, but neither looked toward him as they shared the story. Hannah made Shelby giggle while acting out the story with the stuffed toy. He was witnessing a family coming together, a family that didn't include him.

Three years ago, he'd made his choice to focus on building a business instead of a family. Maybe Hannah was right about him being wrong up until now, but he didn't know how to get off the path he was on when he was so close to making his dream come true. But he was beginning to see the cost of that decision. It was higher than he'd imagined.

Chapter Nine

"Today is moving day, ain't so?" Daniel asked as he walked into the backyard at the Lambright house the following week. He'd stopped by only occasionally since Shelby began trusting Hannah.

Each time he visited, he'd helped Shelby with her therapy, though the little girl wanted her sister to assist her on everything but the stairs. The exercise seemed as special to the little girl as the games of peekaboo she played with him.

That was the way it was supposed to be, but he realized how much he missed being necessary to their little family. He wondered how much longer he'd have an excuse to drop by because Hannah and Shelby now were comfortable with each other. Hannah had fulfilled her side of the bargain, too, by moving the bees.

Hannah motioned him to stay away from the

two white hives. A spot was cleared to one side for the new hive. Two-by-fours were balanced on wooden legs. One side had longer legs so anything placed on the boards would be level in spite of the hill's slope.

She looked lovely in a green dress beneath her black apron. Her beekeeper's hat was in her left hand. Her *kapp* was askew with one pin hanging out at an odd angle, and strands of her honey-gold hair fluttered around her face. Were her lips as sweet as honey? He'd often wondered when he couldn't get Hannah out of his mind and wanted her in his arms again, but kissing her three years ago when he had no intention of offering her marriage would have been all kinds of wrong.

The hushed hum of the bees' wings created an undertone for songs sung by robins somewhere nearby. He drew in a deep breath, almost disappointed when he didn't smell the rich greenness of a fresh-cut hayfield. The sounds were of spring, of days when the sunshine grew warm and *kinder* tossed aside their shoes to curl their toes in the soft, new grass. As he and Hannah had one day near the pond on his family's farm. They'd walked together and skipped stones across the still waters. That day, he'd nearly thrown aside his plans for the future and pulled her to him and kissed her.

"How are the bees doing?" he asked, pushing aside his thoughts.

"So far, they're doing well. It'll change when I bring the other hive up here. They'll be distressed because their hive is close to a strange one." She gave him a wry smile, and he was grateful she didn't sense the course of his thoughts. "You're either brave or foolish to come out here without checking first."

"I did check. Your great-grandmother was eager to tell me where you were." He arched a single brow as he thought of how excited *Gross-mammi* Ella had been, believing he'd come to the house to court her great-granddaughter. He kept the conversation to himself as he did his yearning to hold Hannah close and explore her lips. *Stop thinking of that!* It was easier said than done, so he asked, "Where's Shelby?"

"She's napping. She didn't sleep well last night. She's fussy all day, but her teething pain seems worse at night. Maybe her face hurts more when she's lying down. I rubbed honey on her gums along with a teething gel your brother Amos recommended. The combination helped, and she was asleep before I put her in the crib."

He saw Hannah's exhaustion, but it didn't steal the delicate prettiness that had drawn his eyes to her from the first time he'd seen her. That sunny summer afternoon, he'd been hanging out and jesting with his twin brother…as usual. He and Micah had been having some sort of contest to see which one of them was faster or smarter or whatever…as usual. They'd been with friends who'd been talked into attending the youth gathering by someone's younger sister…as usual.

From the corner of his eye as Micah was making a joke, Daniel had seen a blonde girl in a dark blue dress leaping up to hit a volleyball over the net. She'd succeeded and was instantly surrounded by teammates who congratulated her on her *gut* play. One of the players must have noticed him and his friends approaching. The blonde girl had turned, and his gaze had locked with hers.

He knew nothing would be as usual again.

And it hadn't been. That evening was the first time he'd asked Hannah if he could drive her home. When she'd said *ja*, he'd wondered if he'd ever been so happy. They'd talked about everything and nothing, getting to know each other and feeling—at least in his case—as if he'd known her his whole life. She'd laughed at his humorous stories, and he'd been fascinated by her sparkling brown eyes. In fact, he'd been immersed in joy until the demanding voice of his determination to be his own boss sounded in his mind after he'd dropped Hannah off and continued home.

Today wasn't the first time—nor would it be

the last, he was certain—when he wondered what might have happened if he'd ignored the strident voice and instead listened to his heart. He'd tried, asking her again and again to let him take her home, but the dream of owning a construction company refused to be silenced.

"Poor little tyke," Daniel said when he realized he'd become mired again in his thoughts of the past. "She must have most of her teeth, ain't so?"

"If I counted right, she's got five more to come in." She yawned, putting her hand up to her mouth. "Sorry. When Shelby doesn't sleep, nobody sleeps." Glancing at her hives shadowed by the barn farther up the hill, she sighed. "I know a lot about taking care of bees. I wish I knew as much about taking care of a toddler."

"You didn't plan to become a *mamm* now."

"No, but God has surprises for us." She gave him another crooked grin. "Some more than others."

"You're doing a great job, Hannah."

For a moment, he thought she might protest or demur, but instead she said, "*Danki.* I'm trying to make a home for the three of us."

"Don't you want more?" Maybe if she'd talk about her dreams, she could understand his and why he'd done what he had. Maybe then she'd forgive him…and he'd be able to forgive himself.

"I'm not sure I can handle more, Daniel." She

ran her fingers along the mesh on the front of her mask. "Sometimes being surrounded by peace and quiet so I can be in the moment is the most *wunderbaar* thing I can imagine."

"Do you mean like in Psalm 46? 'Be still, and know that I am God.'"

"*Ja.* I try to surrender up the problems of the day because God knows how to resolve them better than I do."

Her faith wasn't gentle as he'd once thought, but a fierce force propelling her through the challenges of her life. He wished he could be as willing to hand his problems to the Lord. He wanted to, but his impatience got in the way, and he believed he had to move his dreams forward himself. *Mamm* had hinted more than once he should let life unfold as it was meant to in God's plan instead of Daniel trying to make it happen as he wanted it to.

"So what can I do for you, Daniel?" Hannah asked.

"Can't I stop by to see how moving the bees is going?"

"Can you?"

He chuckled. "I guess not. I came to ask a favor. I promise you, if you agree, it won't cost you any more sleep."

"Not losing more sleep sounds lovely. What's the favor?"

"Until today, I don't remember the last time we had a rain-free day." He glanced at the clouds building over the western hills. "And it doesn't look as if it's going to change any time soon. I was wondering if I could put my horse in your barn on rainy days while I'm working on the bridge."

Her eyes widened, and he couldn't help wondering what she'd thought he intended to ask. Maybe it was better he didn't know.

"Of course," she replied. "There's no reason for the poor creature to stand out in the rain. What about the rest of your crew's horses?"

"Two of the men working with us are *Englischers*, and one gives the Amish men on the crew a ride every morning in his truck. Taffy is the only horse at the bridge most of the time."

With a smile, she wagged a finger at him as if he were no older than Shelby. "Make sure you close the barn door. Since it's been raining every day, I've kept the chickens and our two cows in the barn, and I don't want them to wander away."

"I know better than to leave the door open. Just imagine how my big brother Ezra would react. He'd have my hide if I let his prize Brown Swiss cows out." He chuckled. "He watches over them as closely as you do Shelby."

When she laughed, he let the lyrical sound wash over him like a cleansing wave. It swept away the debris left after the decisions he'd made. The dubiousness as he second-guessed himself, the regrets at his mistakes and the invisible scars of hurtful words. Ones he'd spoken and ones spoken to him. Both had been unintentional, but the wound endured nonetheless. And then there was how he'd treated Hannah...

Suddenly he wanted to follow his own advice and leave the past in the past. The best way to do that was to be in the present and look to the future.

"How can I help with moving your bees?"

"I have to do this slowly. If you've got to get to the bridge—"

"We're waiting on an inspection from the county before we can continue. It won't be until tomorrow morning. I sent the other men home. We've got some long days ahead of us to meet our schedule, so they're glad to have a couple hours off this afternoon."

She frowned. "Don't you want to take the afternoon off, too?"

"I am. I'm not working on the bridge. I'm here to help you." He hesitated, then added, "If you can use my help."

His heart threatened to stop beating as he held his breath, waiting for her answer. She had every right to tell him to get lost. Again, he wished he could find the right words to apologize after three years and ask her forgiveness for being a *dummkopf* because he'd been afraid to be honest with her.

"*Danki*, Daniel," she said again. "I could use your help. Shelby won't nap long, I'm sure. I'd like to have this done before she wakes up."

While they walked to the bulkhead, he listened as she outlined what they needed to do. She'd carry a pair of supers to the platform she'd built and set them in place.

"I'll take them out through the bulkhead," she said, "so there's less chance of them escaping into the house."

"So what can I do?"

"Hold the bulkhead door open. I don't want it to fall when I'm coming up. It wouldn't be *gut* for the bees."

"Or for you either." He ran his finger along the thick slab. "This door is heavy. Having it fall on your head would be something you'd notice."

"Even with my hard head?"

He laughed. "I don't know about your head, but even *my* hard head would notice a door crashing on it."

When she giggled, sounding as young and carefree as her little sister, he wanted to capture the sound so he could enjoy it over and over. He'd squandered her musical joy years ago, not realizing how precious it was until her laugh vanished from his life.

He wanted to chastise himself again for being so *dumm*, but it was useless to keep rehashing the past. He couldn't change the man he'd been, the man so focused on his ambitions he couldn't see anything else. So, instead, he helped her remove the quilt and the plywood on top of the supers. Hurrying up the stairs as she donned her veiled hat and plugged the entrances to the supers with some twisted grass, he held on to the heavy door while she brought them into the yard.

She settled the last box filled with honeycomb, the one holding the queen, on top of the other supers. She unplugged the entrances so the bees could fly in and out. Removing her veiled hat again, she smiled. "Having a third hive will mean extra work, but it'll also mean more honey to sell."

"You enjoy working with bees, don't you?"

"I do, and it's partly because I like being my own boss." She sat on the steps by the kitchen door.

"I'd like to be my own boss, too." He sighed and glanced toward the covered bridge. "And if this job goes well, I may be. Finally!"

Hannah was startled by the wistfulness in Daniel's voice. She'd never heard him speak with such honest and deep feelings. While they were walking out together, he'd kept her laughing. She couldn't recall a time when he'd talked about anything important to him or asked her about what mattered to her.

She'd considered him fun to be around and was pleased he'd selected her to take home week after week. Several times, she'd tried to discuss her concerns about how oddly her great-grandmother was acting, but he changed the subject. Only in retrospect had she noticed that. At the time, she'd thought he was trying to tease away her worry. When he'd started flirting with other girls, she'd wondered if she was too serious for someone who loved to laugh as much as he did.

Had she known the real Daniel when they were courting?

That was an unsettling thought. Had Daniel changed, or had she failed to see the real person behind the endless jests?

"I didn't know you wanted to be your own boss," she said when she realized he was waiting for her to respond.

"It's been my goal since I finished school. I'm surprised you're surprised, Hannah."

"Why shouldn't I be surprised? You never mentioned anything about this…before."

He gave her a wry grin. "When a young man

is walking out with a young woman, his attention should be on her. Not his hopes for the future."

"That's maybe the dumbest thing you've ever said to me, Daniel Stoltzfus."

"Really?" His eyes widened in astonishment. "The dumbest?"

She laughed in spite of herself. "If not the dumbest, then close. Why would you think I wouldn't have wanted to know about your hopes and dreams? They're part of you. Isn't that what walking out together is for? To get to know someone well enough to decide if you want to spend the rest of your life with him or her?"

"I thought it was a chance to get a girl alone and maybe steal a kiss."

"You're a rogue!"

"I *was* a rogue. I'm not that guy any longer."

She wasn't sure how to answer. Now wasn't the time to speak of the many rumors she'd heard of his numerous girlfriends who, like her, had believed he was serious and then, after being dropped by him, had married someone else. Not everything shared through the Amish grapevine was true.

"You don't believe me," he said with a grimace. He walked to the bulkhead and lowered the door.

"I didn't say that!"

"You didn't say anything." He sat beside her

on the steps. "Sometimes silence speaks louder than words."

"And actions speak louder than words, too." She wished she hadn't spoken the words as soon as they left her lips.

Beside her, Daniel's face blanched beneath his deep tan. If she'd meant to wound him, she'd succeeded. That hadn't been her aim. Or had it been? Had she intended to hurt him as he'd hurt her years ago? She wanted to take back the words, but wasn't sure how.

Daniel stood and walked away without saying anything else. She got up, too, but didn't follow. What could she say? That what she said wasn't true? It was.

You could apologize, her conscience whispered in her mind.

She took a single step to go after him and ask his forgiveness, but paused when the back door opened.

Grossmammi Ella looked out and called, "Saloma, I can hear your Hannah crying upstairs. She needs her *mamm* with her."

Hannah was tempted to weep right there as her great-grandmother's words warned the old woman was lost in time again. She couldn't leave *Grossmammi* Ella alone with Shelby. Maybe if Hannah ran upstairs, got her little sister and went after Daniel, she could...

The sound of buggy wheels rolling away into the distance warned her it was too late. She sighed, hoping she'd have a chance to say she was sorry. She didn't want their friendship to end again before it'd barely begun.

Chapter Ten

Daniel listened to the rain tapping against the roof of the covered bridge. Was the rain ever going to stop? During the past week, except on the day Hannah had moved her bees, it'd stormed for four days, and it'd been overcast and drizzled the rest. The wind remained as chilly as it'd been a month ago, and the creek beneath the bridge was rising and running faster each day. He'd heard his crew say, half-joking, that they needed to start building an ark.

He was tired of having to rework his schedule around tasks they could accomplish while rain fell. If it sprinkled, he took a chance on running the power tools off the portable generator he'd set on the side of the bridge farther away from the Lambright house. It wasn't the best location, but the bridge, even stripped of the boards on its deck and side walls, muted the generator's noise.

He didn't want the racket to intrude on either Shelby's or *Grossmammi* Ella's afternoon rest.

That none of his crew had mentioned the inconvenience of the generator's position warned him that they'd guessed why he'd made the decision. He wasn't going to ask why they weren't curious. He was just grateful they hadn't questioned him.

He drove the nail into the thick beam which would support the new deck. Working kept him from thinking too much about Hannah and the harsh words she'd thrown at him four days ago. That what she said was true had added to their sting. His actions *had* spoken louder than his words three years ago, because he hadn't said a single word.

"There she goes again! I wonder why she's always in such a hurry when she heads out at this time of day." Phil Botti leaned back to give himself a better view of the road leading out to the old mill which had given the bridge its name. The young man, the son of Jake Botti, the man who'd asked Daniel to supervise the project, was a hard worker, but distracted by every vehicle passing by.

"Who?" Daniel asked as he calculated the proper angle for the next board he should cut to support the bridge's right arch. Each one must be the exact length so each portion of the arch could handle its proper share of the weight of the bridge deck as well as the walls and roof.

"Hannah Lambright."

His head snapped up. What was Hannah doing out on the inclement day? The cold would bother her great-grandmother.

Hearing muffled chuckles, Daniel ignored his crew. Since they'd begun work on the bridge, the Amish men and the *Englischers* had made several comments loud enough so he couldn't miss them. Comments about the amount of time he'd spent at the Lambrights' house and how he had a lighter step when Hannah brought the toddler and her great-grandmother to visit the men working on the bridge. Many of the comments were appreciative of the *kaffi* she shared along with cookies or biscuits dripping with honey from her hives, but he couldn't look past the glances his crew shared while their heads bent toward each other.

There was no need for whispers. He knew what they were talking about. They thought he was courting Hannah. If they had any idea how far it was from the truth, maybe they'd stop. But he wouldn't discuss Hannah with anyone, not even his brothers, though Jeremiah had given him an opening several times since their conversation in Daniel's almost finished house.

Hannah's buggy disappeared along the road

at her horse's fastest pace. She was headed up-stream along the creek and the dead end near the ruins of the mill that hadn't been in use since before he was born. Maybe since before his *daed* had been born.

Why was Hannah going there? The asphalt road changed to gravel and then to dirt less than a half mile beyond the Jones farm. The dirt must have turned into mire after so much rain. She could get stuck out there.

He'd seen her rush away in her buggy at least four times in the last two weeks. It was, he realized, always about three in the afternoon. Right around the time when Hannah's great-grandmother finished her nap and came out of her bedroom. Each time when Hannah had sped away, the buggy had returned to the house less than fifteen minutes later.

His brows dropped into a frown as he stood. "I'll be right back."

He ran after the buggy. It would take too long to hitch his horse, and he wanted answers.

Now.

She should be used to this nonsense, Hannah told herself, but she couldn't become accustomed to discovering her great-grandmother had wandered away from the house again without saying where she was going. Not that there was any need. *Grossmammi* Ella went only two places on her own. Either to the barn where she called for cows that hadn't been there in a decade, or she headed toward the old mill. Hannah had no idea why her great-grandmother went there, and the elderly woman couldn't explain.

Grossmammi Ella always acted baffled when they returned to the house, and Hannah wasn't sure if her great-grandmother knew why she was outside. Each time she became lost in her memories seemed to go on longer. Would her great-grandmother eventually have an episode when she never returned to the present? Hannah didn't know what she'd do then. Would she have to pretend to be her *mamm* for the rest of her life?

Beside her on the buggy seat, Shelby played with Buzz-buzz. Oh, how Hannah wished she could be like her little sister, caught up in the joys of being a *kind*! Sudden tears rushed into her eyes as she realized, if *Grossmammi* Ella's past continued to overwhelm her, Shelby might never know their real great-grandmother. That was so sad because unless *Daed* returned, the little girl wouldn't have memories of him either.

Was it worse to have someone in your life and lose them, or never to have a single memory of them? Though she tried to halt her thoughts, Daniel appeared in her mind. If she had the choice, would she prefer to have had a crush on him and lost him or to have never known him at all?

She was being preposterous. He'd walked away from her *again* just a few days ago. Exactly as she'd expected, but it didn't make the pain of him leaving any easier.

Hannah saw her great-grandmother standing under a tree and looking along the creek that was higher than it'd been the last time they'd come along the road. What was *Grossmammi* Ella staring at? Nothing was out there but the tumble-down walls of the old mill and the dam built to collect water to make the wheel turn.

Pulling gently on Thunder's reins, Hannah waited for the black horse to halt. Like Hannah, the horse was growing accustomed to these wild drives.

She jumped out, leaving the door open so she could keep an eye on Shelby, and walked through the rain to where the elderly woman stood. "*Grossmammi* Ella?"

Hannah repeated her great-grandmother's name several times before. *Grossmammi* Ella turned to face her. As her eyes focused, bafflement filled them.

"I think you've walked far enough today." Hannah didn't let her smile slide away. "Let's go home. I'll make tea, and I've got your favorite cookies."

Her great-grandmother didn't answer. She kept staring at Hannah as if she didn't recognize her.

"*Grossmammi* Ella," she pleaded, "we need to get out of the rain. You'll catch a cold. You don't want to get a cold, do you?"

The old woman remained silent.

Hannah wasn't sure what to do. Touching her great-grandmother when she was lost in the past could bring on her uncontrollable temper. That was how Hannah got struck the day before yesterday. Her ear still hurt from the blow.

But they couldn't stand out in the rain, getting drenched. Shelby must be getting chilled, too. They needed to go home.

Calling the old woman's name again was futile. *Grossmammi* Ella didn't respond or move.

"Da-dan!" cried Shelby with excitement.

When Hannah saw Daniel coming around the buggy, she was torn between being relieved he'd chased after her and dismay that he was witnessing how out-of-control her life had become. She wasn't making any progress persuading her great-grandmother to get in the buggy now that it had stopped raining. Maybe he could. She couldn't allow her frustration to prevent her from accepting help.

Greeting Shelby with a laugh and tickling the little girl who adored him, he turned to Hannah and *Grossmammi* Ella. "You're going to get stuck if you let the buggy sit there much longer. The wheels are already sinking into the mud."

"I know." Exasperation sharpened Hannah's voice, and she took a steadying breath to calm herself. Her great-grandmother became unreasonable if Hannah showed aggravation. "We're leaving."

Grossmammi Ella startled her by saying, "I'm not going." Her great-grandmother crossed her arms over her chest and glared at her and Daniel.

Stepping past Hannah, he went to the elderly woman. He was smiling as if none of them had a care in the world. "*Grossmammi* Ella," he said in his charming voice that seemed to work with women of every age, "you know it's time for Hannah to start getting supper ready. What will we do if we don't have anything to eat after a hard day's work?"

"We? You're coming to supper at our house?" The old woman turned to scowl at Hannah. "Why didn't you tell me you'd invited him?"

"I…" She refused to lie to her great-grandmother, but saying *Grossmammi* Ella was confused would make the situation worse.

"Oh, I shouldn't have said anything," Daniel said with his easy grin. "I guess Hannah wanted it to be a surprise."

"For all of us."

"Let me help you into the buggy, *Grossmammi*

Ella." Before turning to her great-grandmother, Daniel whispered, "I'm sorry, Hannah."

Shocked at the words she'd come to doubt that she'd ever hear from him, she watched as he assisted the elderly woman to step into the buggy. He made sure she had a blanket over her knees before he closed the door.

When he faced her, Hannah made sure her astonishment was well hidden.

"*Danki* for convincing her to get into the buggy."

"I wasn't sure I could when she knew who I was. It helps when she believes I'm her late husband." He grimaced. "That sounds pretty lousy, but you know what I mean."

"I do."

"Does she always know who you are?"

Instead of answering, because she didn't want to raise his suspicions further given that her great-grandmother was barely holding on to her mind, she said, "Like you said, we need to move the buggy before it settles farther into the mud."

"Avoiding my questions isn't going to change anything, Hannah."

"Can't we discuss this some other time? I want to get my great-grandmother and my little sister home before it starts raining again."

"All right." His reluctance laced through the two words. As he walked with her around the buggy to the driver's side, he glanced over at the old stone mill which had lost its roof in a long-forgotten storm. "What does *Grossmammi* Ella find so interesting about the mill?"

"I don't have any idea, and she won't tell me." She shuddered. "I wish I knew, because maybe I could convince her not to come out here. It's dangerous with the slippery banks around the mill pond. The old dam should have washed out long ago."

He nodded as he opened the buggy door. "When I was over at Jake Botti's office, he talked about other projects that need to be done in the county. The dam is high on the list of priority repairs, but I don't know when the county supervisors plan to get to it. Look how bad the bridge had to get before they decided to fix it." He motioned for her to climb in. "I wasn't joking. You'd better get the buggy moving before it's stuck here until the road dries out."

Hannah didn't hesitate. Getting in, she left the door open as she slapped the reins on Thunder's back and gave him the order to start. He pulled, but the buggy didn't move. Straining again, he tried to walk forward. She halted him, not wanting the horse to hurt himself. She frowned when she felt the wheels drop more deeply into the thick mud.

"You're definitely stuck." Daniel put one foot

on the buggy's step. "I hate to ask this, but you need to get out."

He was right. She was so frustrated she wanted to cry. Now she had to persuade *Grossmammi* Ella to get out.

Again Daniel succeeded where she couldn't. Hannah held Shelby close as he talked the old woman into stepping down. When she stood beside Hannah, he went to Thunder. He gripped the reins and spoke to the horse.

Thunder shook his mane as if agreeing with whatever Daniel said, then stepped forward. One step. A second one. The mud released the buggy's wheels with a sucking sound. Once the wheels emerged from the mud, Thunder moved quickly a few more paces. It was as if the black horse knew how important it was not to let the buggy wheels get bogged again.

"Let's go!" Daniel waved for them to get into the buggy before it sank into the mire again.

Hannah got in and held Shelby on her lap as he assisted her great-grandmother. *Grossmammi* Ella stared at Thunder as if the horse was the most fascinating thing she'd ever seen. Daniel grabbed the reins and gave the horse the command to go.

The drive to the house would have been silent except for Shelby's "talking." She kept patting

Daniel's arm, and Hannah realized the little girl had missed him.

As Hannah had.

What's wrong with me? He acts outrageously, so I should be glad he's not at the house every day. But her days had seemed emptier and longer and flavorless since he'd stormed off after helping her move the bees.

At the house, Hannah helped her great-grandmother inside while Daniel unhitched the horse and put him in the barn. *Grossmammi* Ella sat in her favorite chair as if nothing had happened. Shelby toddled to the box of toys in a corner of the kitchen. Sitting on the floor, she took Buzzbuzz out and hugged the stuffed bee.

Everything was as it should be, but Hannah's nerves were on edge. She wrapped her arms around herself when she heard the back door open and Daniel enter. Going into the kitchen, she thanked him for helping with her great-grandmother.

"I'm here every workday, Hannah." He was as serious and appeared as uncomfortable as she did. "My buggy is here, and, if you let me know when she's gone roaming again, I can go and bring her back faster than you can get Shelby and give chase."

"I can't ask you to do that. You've got your job to do."

"The foreman has the right to a *kaffi* break each day."

"It's supposed to be your time to relax so you can finish the rest of the day's work. It's not your time to be running off after my great-grandmother."

He folded his arms over his chest, drawing her gaze to its breadth. She looked away because she didn't want to be distracted by that enticing sight. It brought reminders of her cheek resting against the spot where his chest and shoulder met.

"You make it sound," he said in a taut voice, "as if you sit around doing nothing. I know as the weather gets warmer, you'll be busier with your bees as well as other chores. I may not have time to go after your great-grandmother, but neither do you."

"But she's *my* responsibility."

"If you don't want my help..." His words trailed away.

She knew what she should say. *Of course, I'd appreciate your help.* That was what plain folk did for each other. They lent a helping hand so nobody's burden was too great. The silence stretched between them, becoming almost painful, as she sought the right words to say.

Again she didn't have a chance because he reached for the knob on the door. "I thought we could be friends."

"I thought so, too." Why were words failing her? Maybe because she couldn't say what she wanted to. She shouldn't speak of how, after breaking her heart, he'd started to help it heal. That would reveal too much. He'd think she was crazy when he'd made it clear—over and over—his dreams of the future didn't include her. "Maybe it's impossible for us to be friends, Daniel."

His brows rose, and she knew her blunt words had shocked him. But to tiptoe around the truth would only hurt them again. She couldn't risk that.

Twisting the knob, he yanked the door open. "Well, if you need me, Hannah, you know where I am."

Then he was gone again, and she was left there by herself...again.

Chapter Eleven

From where he stood by the covered bridge, Daniel recognized the small red car heading away from Hannah's house. It belonged to Todd Howland, the speech therapist who came twice a week to work with Shelby. Unlike with physical therapy and occupational therapy, there weren't exercises Daniel could help with, so there was no need for him to go to the house.

Even if he was sure Hannah wouldn't slam the door in his face.

Why had he made such a muddle of everything with her? She'd agreed to be his friend, and he should be glad she had. Instead, he seemed to be doing everything he could to irritate her.

Why?

It didn't make sense, especially when he'd been enjoying time with her and Shelby. So why had he said things he knew would upset her?

He pulled his gaze from the car as it turned a corner and disappeared from sight. All last night, rain had poured through the openings in the bridge roof that had been made wider by the storm's strong winds. Tomorrow morning, sheets of plywood were being delivered from the lumberyard. He'd hoped they could get the boards to him today, but it'd been impossible. Once the wood arrived, he and his crew would get up on the rotting roof and tack on the sheets to stop the leaks until they had time to replace the shingles. It was beyond the scope of the job he'd been hired to do, but he hoped the project still could be done on time. That was important, so he could use Jake Botti as a reference for a couple of other jobs he wanted to bid on.

Before he could think of fixing the whole roof, however, more of the bridge's deck must be finished. There wasn't any place to put a ladder now with the whole deck removed.

Crossing his arms, he sighed. Nothing had gone as he'd planned. The weather refused to cooperate, and it seemed for every day they managed to work, two were lost to rain. As soon as the first half dozen boards were back in place on the deck, the saw used to cut the planks could be set up out of the rain.

No rain tomorrow, Lord. He almost laughed at his prayer. No doubt the farmers in the county were praying the rain returned to water the seeds they sowed today.

Or were they able to get out in their wet fields to work? He looked at the swollen creek. Like others near Paradise Springs, it was running too fast, too high, and was the color of *kaffi* with too much milk.

He wasn't going to get any more work done today. He might as well spend the time finishing the baseboard molding at his house. He was astonished to realize he hadn't gone to the house in over a week. Longer, because the last time he'd spent time there was before he'd helped Hannah move her bees. He needed to get back to it because his twin brother had mentioned a youth gathering tonight, and how he planned to ask a special girl if he could take her home.

A prickle of envy spurred Daniel off the bridge. His brother's relationship with Katie Kay, nebulous as it might be, was simpler than his with Hannah. After three years of convincing himself he'd done the right thing by not getting serious with her, he was the one having trouble being just friends. His thoughts kept urging him to draw her into his arms.

"Your dream is to have your own company," he chided himself as he walked to the Lambrights' barn where he stabled Taffy every day.

Stuffing his hands in his coat pockets, he felt

the crackle of the piece of paper he'd shoved in there before he left home. *Mamm* had given him a message for Hannah and her great-grandmother. She'd written it down because she'd said she didn't want him to forget the details while his mind was on boards and nails for the covered bridge. That is what she'd said, but her laughter-filled eyes suggested she thought he'd lose every thought in his head the moment he spoke to Hannah.

If Hannah was surprised to see him at her front door, she gave no sign. Daniel couldn't guess if she was pleased or annoyed he'd come to the house. She wiped her hands on a dish towel as she stepped aside to let him in. Past her, he saw her little sister and her great-grandmother looking at a cloth book together in the kitchen.

For the first time, Shelby hadn't come running to him. That startled him and made him sad. It was for the best, he told himself, that Shelby was feeling comfortable with her family. Still, he missed her enthusiastic greetings and her contralto laughter.

The aroma of chocolate swept over him, and he wondered if Hannah was baking that special chocolate chip cake she'd brought to youth events while they'd walked out together. The rich cake with its peanut butter icing had been a favorite with the young people, and Hannah had made sure she saved an extra piece for him to enjoy on the way home. She'd made a whole chocolate chip cake for him for his twenty-second birthday that year.

The week before he turned his back on her.

Shame rushed through him, but how could he ask for her forgiveness when he'd told everyone—including himself—over and over that the past was in the past and they needed to focus on the future?

Pride, warned his conscience. He was being prideful.

"I came by," he said, ignoring his conscience, "because *Mamm* asked me to invite you and *Grossmammi* Ella to a quilting frolic the day after tomorrow at our place. She says she remembers your great-grandmother used to be one of the finest quilters in the county."

"Tell her *danki*, but I doubt we'll be able to go." She kept wiping her hands on the towel, and he knew she was nervous and wanted the conversation over.

He frowned. "You don't have to turn down the invitation because of how you feel about me. *Mamm* is asking you."

"I realize that."

"So go if you want to."

"Go where?" asked *Grossmammi* Ella as she came into the living room. Her eyes lit up.

Did she see him today as Daniel Stoltzfus or as her late husband?

He got his answer when the elderly woman went on, "Daniel, have you come to ask our Hannah to walk out with you?"

"No, *Grossmammi* Ella. *Mamm* wanted me to stop by with an invitation for you and Hannah to come to a quilt frolic at our house the day after tomorrow."

"A quilt frolic?"

For a moment, Daniel thought the old woman wasn't sure what he meant, that she'd forgotten how, when the Amish gathered to work together, they called it a frolic. He sought the right words to explain without insulting her.

Before he could, *Grossmammi* Ella turned to Hannah. "Do you know where my sewing box is?"

"Ja," she answered. "Do you want me to get it?"

"Not now, but I'll need it for the frolic. And my reading glasses? Do you know where they are?"

Hannah looked as stunned as if someone had announced Amish women were expected to drive bright red Ferraris. She gulped before replying, *"Ja.* I know where they are. On the table by your bed, but we aren't going—"

"Of course, we're going." *Grossmammi* Ella's brows lowered. "I thought I'd taught you better, Hannah! When a neighbor announces a frolic, it's our chance to offer assistance to them. And we'll learn the latest news in the district."

"It's not today," Hannah said when her great-grandmother paused to take a breath. "That's what I was going to say."

"Well, you should have said it then." The old woman walked from the living room, her head held high.

Daniel put his hand over his mouth to hide his smile. He was glad he did because *Grossmammi* Ella paused and turned to him.

"What are you waiting for?" the old woman asked.

"Me?" He glanced at Hannah and saw she was as puzzled as he was.

"*Ja.* You! Are all young men as dense as you are? They weren't when I was a girl. They could see it's a nice day, just right for taking a young woman for a walk. So why aren't you asking our Hannah to go for a walk? She's a kind young woman who takes *gut* care of her old great-grandmother. What more could you ask for than our Hannah's company on this pretty day the *gut* Lord has made, Daniel Stoltzfus?"

He wasn't sure which question to answer first, except he knew it wouldn't be the last one. Without looking at Hannah, he knew her cheeks had become the adorable pink painted by her strongest emotions.

"Hannah is busy with her bees." It was a lame answer, but it was the best he could manage.

Grossmammi Ella wrinkled her nose. "The bees can take care of themselves for an hour, and so can I. You should take our Hannah out in the sunshine and enjoy the day. So what are you waiting for?"

Hannah wished she could blame *Grossmammi* Ella's questions on dementia, but it was clear the elderly woman knew where and when she was and what she was asking. Poor Daniel! He hadn't anticipated any matchmaking when he came to deliver his *mamm*'s invitation. Hannah was still irritated with him, but she had to pity him when he confronted her great-grandmother.

"*Grossmammi* Ella," she said, "I can't go for a walk. I need to watch Shelby."

A frustrated yelp came from the kitchen. Whirling, Hannah stared at little Shelby trying to get her hair unstuck from her fingers. Strands clung to her cheeks. The front of her pinafore was covered with globs of honey.

"Like you've been doing now?" Her great-grandmother sniffed. "Take the *boppli* with you. She could use some sunshine, too. I don't know what's going on with youngsters nowadays. In my day, we enjoyed a spring stroll."

The old woman walked away, going into her bedroom and shutting the door so neither Hannah nor Daniel had a chance to reply.

Hannah looked at Daniel's shocked expression and burst into laughter. She clamped her hands over her mouth to keep her great-grandmother from hearing, but her shoulders shook with mirth. Soon Daniel was trying to restrain himself, too.

Deciding the best way to stop laughing was to do something, Hannah went to where Shelby sat. The little girl had pulled herself up onto the chair before digging into the bottle of honey, spreading it everywhere.

Daniel stepped past her and picked up the *kind.* He held her out straight-armed, so her sticky clothes and fingers couldn't reach him. "Time for a bath, my girl."

Hannah hurried ahead of them into the bathroom and began to run water into the tub. As she got a washcloth and soap, Daniel undressed her little sister. He asked where Hannah wanted the honey-coated clothes, and she pointed to a bucket near the door.

"My mop bucket will do," she said.

Lifting Shelby high in the air, Daniel set her in the water and began washing the sticky streaks off her hands and arms. Hannah sat on her heels and watched. So much had changed since the first time she and Daniel had put the *kind* in the tub. Shelby didn't cringe away when Hannah touched her. Maybe it was because Hannah felt confident around the little girl. She no longer feared she would do something wrong and hurt the toddler.

However, one thing—one important thing—hadn't changed. Shelby adored Daniel. She babbled her version of his name as he shampooed her hair. Slapping her hands in the water, she giggled when Daniel pretended to be horrified to get wet.

Her lingering anger faded as Hannah watched them. She couldn't act as if Daniel was a horrible person who thought only of himself. For too long, she'd focused on a single selfish act and refused to think about the *gut* things he'd done. She'd been as self-centered as she'd accused him of being.

But if she didn't have her anger as a bulwark against him, how could she protect her heart from being hurt again? There must be a way. *Dearest Lord, help me discover it, so I no longer harbor this animosity within me. I don't want to tote around this burden any longer.*

Hannah toweled off the clean *kind* and then redressed her. Brushing out Shelby's soft, golden hair, she braided it.

"Ready?" asked Daniel as she folded the damp towel over the side of the tub.

"For what?"

"Our walk."

Again, heat soared up her face. "You don't have to go for a walk with me because *Grossmammi* Ella told you to."

"She didn't tell me to. She asked me why I wasn't asking you to go. I'm asking you *and* Shelby if you'd like to go for a walk. We may find some early flowers along the road."

"We will."

"You sound sure."

"No, I sound like a beekeeper. I've seen my bees working hard for the past couple of days."

He winked at Shelby before asking, "Shall we follow the *beezzzz*?" He stretched out the sound until the little girl giggled and made the buzzing sound that made them all laugh.

"How can I say no to both of you?" Hannah asked.

"That was the idea." This time, his wink was for her.

Something quivered deep in her heart, and, for the first time in too long, she didn't try to silence a pulse of honest joy. She did want to call Daniel her friend. No, she wanted far more than friendship with him, but she wasn't going to make the same mistake of letting her heart overrule her head.

She continued to savor her happiness as she pulled on her coat and bonnet while Daniel helped her little sister into her coat. Shelby kept her fingers in her mouth, a sign that her gums hurt. Hannah dabbed honey and teething gel on them. Shelby's last new tooth couldn't come in soon enough.

When the three of them stepped out into the backyard, the hives were alive with the sound of bees. Shelby began copying the sound and giggling.

"It's astonishing how much noise those little wings can make," Daniel said. "I can hear it in my bones as well as my ears."

"There are a lot of little wings," Hannah replied with a smile. "One hive can hold as many as fifty thousand bees."

He whistled a long, steady note before saying, "I had no idea that many lived in a single hive. But they've got the right idea. Let's not waste this sunny day. We haven't had many lately."

Hannah held Shelby's right hand as they walked down the sloping yard. The little girl reached for Daniel, but her arms were too short. When they got to the road, he picked her up. Setting her on his shoulders, he clasped her hands and bounced along the road like a runaway pony. Shelby squealed with delight.

Following at a more sedate pace, Hannah watched how careful Daniel was with the little girl. He didn't jostle her too hard, but kept her laughing. Someday, when he decided to settle down, he would be a *gut* father.

Halfway between her home and her neighbor's, where a small thicket of blackberry bushes and saplings grew, she paused and bent to look at clumps of snowdrops perched atop their green stems. The blossoms drooped toward the ground, making the ground beneath the bushes look as if there had been a fresh fall of snow. She called to Daniel to bring Shelby to look at them.

The little girl was delighted. Hannah convinced her to pick only a couple, telling her the bees would want the rest.

"I'm not sure how much she understands," Hannah said, glancing at Daniel who was squatting beside the *kind*.

Shelby looked at her and made the buzzing sound. When Hannah smiled, the little girl grinned, showing off her newest tooth.

"I'd say she knows what you're saying." Daniel stood and brushed his hands against this trousers. "Do you think there was a house here at one time and someone planted these flowers?"

"Maybe. Or the seeds were scattered here by birds."

"Look here." He reached deeper into the bushes. "Bloodroot." He pulled up one, and the sap burst out onto his fingers, turning them red. "My brothers and I used to use these to paint the trees. It takes a lot of them to write Daniel Paul Stoltzfus on bark."

"They're too pretty to yank from the ground. Look at the yellow in the center."

When he walked into the thicket, where the shadows draped the ground in cool dampness, Hannah took her little sister's hand and went, too. They had to stop every few steps as they climbed the slope so Shelby could collect another blossom. Hannah doubted there would be much left of the flowers by the time they returned to the house because the toddler clutched the stems tightly, and her bouquet already sagged over her tiny fingers.

The sound of trickling water reached Hannah's ears before she saw a spring half-hidden by thick moss. Daniel paused and then dropped to sit by the narrow stream of water drifting beneath the bare roots of the nearby trees.

Drawing Shelby onto his lap, he handed her a leaf that had fallen last autumn. He laughed when the little girl tossed it toward the water. She missed, so he stretched to retrieve it. On her second try, it landed in the small stream. She clapped her hands in glee as the leaf twirled and spun on the current before disappearing beyond the roots.

Hannah smiled when Daniel stood, and she took Shelby's hand again. They walked out of the shadows into the sunshine. When Shelby held up her arms and teased, he put the little girl on his shoulders again.

"You're going to spoil her," Hannah said with a laugh.

"I hope so." He winked before galloping across the open field.

Again she watched the two of them and couldn't help smiling. She was glad she hadn't accepted Daniel's offer to take Shelby to live at his house, but she was happy he'd helped during the rough times until her little sister began to trust her.

When Daniel bent, he set Shelby on her feet. He plucked a long piece of grass. "Listen to this." He blew on it. Hard.

An awkward sounding squeak emerged.

Shelby clapped her hands before holding them out. He squatted beside her again and helped her put her fingers around the piece of grass. Holding it close to her mouth, he urged her to blow on it. The little girl did, and the faintest sound emerged.

Hannah cheered before picking another piece of grass. When she held it to her lips, a lovely note rippled through the air.

Daniel stared at her wide-eyed, then applauded. Shelby did, too.

Bowing, Hannah tossed the grass aside and hugged Shelby as her little sister ran to throw her arms around Hannah's legs. She didn't look in Daniel's direction, not wanting him to see how much she wished she could embrace him, too.

"Hey! Look!" He pointed toward the sky that was littered with thickening clouds. "There's a bald eagle."

Hannah held her breath as she watched the magnificent bird soar overhead. Its motions looked effortless while it drifted, letting the winds high above them carry it.

"It's beautiful," she whispered.

"I'm glad whenever I see an eagle." He walked over to stand by her and Shelby. "We almost lost them."

"But people wised up in time to bring them back from extinction."

"Too bad being smart doesn't happen more often. We don't realize our mistakes until we look back at our lives and know we should have chosen better."

When his gaze caught hers, she couldn't look away from the powerful emotions within it. He wasn't talking about birds. He was talking about him and her.

She searched his face, her gaze lingering on the cleft in his chin he despised and she thought made his face interesting. Again the longing to step into his embrace and let his arms close around her was so strong she had to fight herself.

She didn't want to talk about the past. It was dangerous territory. As the future was. That was why she preferred to think about the here and now. Except as his blue eyes regarded her, the moment itself held the potential for disaster.

Picking up Shelby, she set the *kind* on her hip. "*Grossmammi* Ella will get worried if we stay out past the time she gets up. We need to go."

"Hannah—"

She didn't let him finish. She left with Shelby. She was being a coward, turning away from the problem instead of facing it. But she knew where courage would lead.

To her heart being broken all over again.

Chapter Twelve

Hannah was amazed two days later when *Grossmammi* Ella asked her when they'd be leaving for the Stoltzfus farm.

"As soon as breakfast is done," Hannah replied, hoping her shock wasn't visible. For the past six months, she'd had to insist every church Sunday that her great-grandmother leave the house and attend services. A few times, *Grossmammi* Ella had been so stubborn neither she nor Hannah had been able to go.

But the elderly woman acted as excited as Shelby did when she had a cookie. *Grossmammi* Ella talked about the many quilting frolics she'd attended and spoke of people Hannah had never met. Hoping her great-grandmother continued to focus on the present, Hannah packed their sewing boxes in the buggy and made sure Shelby had Buzz-buzz with her.

As they drove onto the creek road, Hannah heard shouts and the whir of power tools from the covered bridge. Knowing she should pay no attention to the men working on it, she couldn't keep from looking in that direction. Men were cutting boards and nailing them in place to create a new deck. She picked out Daniel as if a flashlight focused on him. Her breath caught when he began to climb a ladder, balancing a large sheet of plywood on his back.

Don't fall. Don't fall. Don't fall. The words resonated through her mind as she drew in the reins to watch while he climbed through a hole in the bridge's roof and set the plywood down.

She released her breath and urged Thunder to continue along the road. She should be grateful that Daniel would be occupied at the bridge so she didn't have to see him at his family's farm. Since their walk through the woods and meadow, she hadn't been able to get his easy grin and warm gaze out of her mind. He'd slipped into her dreams again.

Her hands tightened on the reins until the leather cut into her palms. She was close to making the same mistake. Friendship! That was all they could share, and she must not pray for more.

Hannah was relieved when traffic demanded her attention as she reached the center of Paradise Springs. It kept her from thinking of anything else. They had to wait several minutes to cross Route 30 because cars and tractor-trailers rushed by at a speed far over the posted speed limit in the village.

"Is that where Daniel works?" asked *Grossmammi* Ella when they passed a low building with the sign Stoltzfus Family Shops in the parking lot.

"I don't know."

Her great-grandmother gave her a baffled glance, and Hannah kept her gaze on the road and the cars passing them. Why didn't she know more about the man who'd infiltrated her dreams? Did he work there with his brothers? She'd never gone to any of the shops except the grocery store.

Hannah was relieved when they reached the Stoltzfus farmhouse. It was set off a long lane. A half dozen buggies were parked under the trees that would give the house cooling shade in the summer. The house, like the barns, was painted white. In a nearby field, a team of five mules pulled a plow. *Englisch* farmers had to wait for the ground to dry out so their tractors didn't get mired in the fields, but plain farmers who used horses and mules were already at work getting ready for planting.

Wanda Stoltzfus met them at the kitchen door and ushered them in as if they were special guests. She introduced them to her current daughters-in-law and her future one. Finding *Grossmammi* Ella a seat at the middle of the quilting frame where she'd be able to hear what everyone said as they worked, she urged Hannah to sit beside her great-grandmother. Shelby was bundled away to play with the other *kinder* who were too young for school and were being overseen by Daniel's younger sister Esther who showed the earliest signs of being pregnant.

Hannah didn't mention it, but others weren't so circumspect. The young woman, who'd been the district's schoolteacher until her marriage, was congratulated and teased by the other women. Everyone had an opinion on whether the *boppli* would be a boy or a girl. Esther smiled as she went into the other room to entertain the *kinder*.

The day passed quickly as Hannah worked with eight other women on the large Sunshine and Shadow quilt stretched between them on the quilt frame. She tried to match her great-grandmother's tiny stitches. The small squares in light and dark shades of blue, purple and green created a large diamond in the middle of the quilt. The border, which was more than a foot wide, was dark green and edged with a narrow strip of navy blue fabric.

As she listened to the conversations around

her, she wondered again why she'd let *Gross-mammi* Ella's condition keep them from spending time with their neighbors. Her great-grandmother seemed more alive than she had in months as news from the district was shared. Hannah heard the names of several friends from her school years. Shelby joined them when the quilters took a break for a lunch of salads and sandwiches and pies of every description made by their hostess and her family. Hannah hoped it wouldn't be long before the Lambright family could become a vital part of the community again.

Weaving his way through the crowd of women getting ready to go home and make the evening meal for their families, Daniel saw Hannah moving toward the kitchen door. He didn't want her to leave yet. He'd cleaned up in the barn, keeping an eye on the house to make sure she didn't go before he'd washed off the sweat of working on the bridge.

"Hannah?"

She glanced over her shoulder and smiled. "Hi, Daniel!"

His heart thudded like a nail gun. He hadn't been sure if she'd talk to him after she'd taken off like a shingle in a high wind the other day. Aware of the women around him, including those from his family, he made sure no tremor tainted his voice as he asked, "Would you like to come and see the project I've been working on for the past year?"

"Where is it?"

"A short walk from here. Get Shelby, and we'll head over. It shouldn't take more than a few minutes." He didn't add he hoped she'd stay longer.

Conflicting emotions flitted through her eyes, and he wasn't sure what she'd decide until she nodded. "Let me get Shelby and her coat. I'll tell *Grossmammi* Ella we'll be right back."

He watched as she did and kissed her great-grandmother on the cheek. *Grossmammi* Ella was so enthralled in telling a story, she didn't seem to notice. Buttoning her coat as well as the *kind*'s, Hannah walked out the door with him.

"You don't need a coat," Daniel said. "It's warmer today than I expected."

"That's what we get when the sky isn't filled with rain clouds." Hannah settled Shelby in her arms, then relinquished her when the toddler held out her arms to Daniel.

He led the way toward the barn. "Watch where you step. Ezra's been trying out some goats to see if they'll eat the weeds along the fence. They've been wandering free."

"The weeds?"

Laughing, he said, "I'm not going to dignify that with an answer. I'm going to enjoy the nice weather."

"The nice weather is frustrating my bees. The weather is warm, but, except for the earliest flowers, most buds haven't burst yet. The bees visit bushes and hedgerows, but come back without much nectar."

"At least, they've got last year's honey to eat." He held the gate open for her and followed her into the field.

She smiled as Shelby bopped her on the head with Buzz-buzz. "Adult bees don't eat honey. They make honey to feed their larvae. Adult bees eat pollen and nectar from blossoms. They store food for themselves, but it seems that as we prefer vegetables from the garden to what we freeze and can, they're eager to get fresh food." With a laugh, she said, "Probably more than you want to know."

"You find it fascinating, and when you talk about it, you make it fascinating for everyone else, too."

"Not everyone. I've encountered plenty of people whose eyes glaze over with boredom when I start prattling on and on about my bees."

With a chuckle, he said, "I've seen the same thing when I start talking about trusses and foundations and sheetrock."

"Well, I can understand that. Nobody in their right mind should get excited about sheetrock."

"*I* get excited about it."

When she arched her brows, he wanted to put his arm around her shoulders and squeeze her. Usually Hannah was the epitome of a proper Amish woman, but he preferred when, like tonight, she was sassy and matched him jest for jest.

"Okay," he said. "Point taken. You wouldn't be the first one to tell me I'm *ab in kopp*. Not even the first today."

"Who called you crazy?"

"Some of the men on my crew. They think I'm crazy to want to replace the whole roof of the Hunter's Mill Creek Bridge when we weren't hired to do that."

She became serious. "But you were hired to fix the bridge, and you can't fix the bridge if the roof's leaking, ain't so?"

"Why do you get it and they don't?"

"Because I'm not the one having to get on the roof?" Her smile returned.

He grinned at her. "Point taken again." Taking a deep breath, he said, "This way."

The woods were dim because the trees blocked the last rays of the early sunset. It would be weeks before the sun was above the horizon after supper. When the *Englischers* went to daylight savings time, he must remember the difference between it and what the Amish called slow time. He wasn't sure why the *Englischers* moved their clocks one hour ahead each spring. He was as impatient for summer to come each year as they were, but the shift didn't make sense to him.

A short distance later, he stepped from the woods and into the clearing. He swept one arm toward the house he'd been working on for so long, but his gaze was focused on Hannah as he asked, "What do you think?"

His heart seemed to stop in midbeat as he waited for her answer. Until that moment, he hadn't realized how important her opinion was to him. More important than anyone else's. He didn't want to think why, so he watched her face, looking for any sign of what she'd say.

Hannah didn't answer right away. Instead she admired the white house in front of her. It was smaller than the rambling farmhouse where his family lived. However, it was freshly painted, and the setting among the trees was idyllic. A pair of large windows flanked the simple wood door. Upstairs, two more windows were set into identical dormers.

"Whose house is this?" she asked.

"Mine. I'm building it."

"Why?" She couldn't ask the next question

burning on her tongue. A man usually built a house when he planned to marry. Had she misread everything? Was Daniel planning to marry another woman?

"I want to use it with prospective clients as an example of the work I—and my construction company—can do."

Relief flooded her. "What a *gut* idea! Can I see inside?"

"I'd hoped you'd want to." He grinned like a kid with a new scooter.

Hannah followed him onto the porch. It was wider than hers, wide enough for chairs where someone could sit and listen to the birds singing good-night.

When he opened the door, he gestured for her to go in first. She did and stared about in astonishment. It was a plain house with no extra ornamentation, but that made it easier for her to see the quality of Daniel's work. Not a single gap showed along the woodwork or the stones on the fireplace. The wood floors glistened and were so smooth they looked like an ice-coated pond.

Daniel set Shelby down, and the toddler headed for the kitchen. Following her, because she wasn't sure what tools might be out there, Hannah stopped as she saw that room. The cabinets were beautiful, and light poured into the room, making the pale yellow walls glow.

"I added skylights for the kitchen and upstairs bathroom," Daniel said in a whisper, "because the trees block much of the sunshine early in the morning and during the later afternoon." He gave her a tentative smile, and she realized he was anxious to know if she liked the house he'd built. "I didn't want to cut more trees than I had to."

"I agree," she said as she watched his shoulders lose their rigid line. "You did this all yourself?"

"*Ja.* While I was working with plumbers and sheetrockers and painters on other jobs, I watched what they did. I asked questions. Lots of them, and I learned their tricks of the trade. What I learned I put to use here." He leaned against the doorframe. "I'll use it until my twin brother, Micah, gets married."

"You'd give your brother a *house* as a wedding gift?" She wondered how she could have considered Daniel selfish and self-centered.

"He'll need it. Why wouldn't I give it to him?"

Walking away and pretending to be fascinated by an arch leading from the kitchen to the laundry room, she asked in what she hoped was a casual voice, "So you don't plan on marrying?"

"I told you, Hannah, I needed to concentrate on starting my business. It wouldn't be fair to spend all my time on that if I were a husband and *daed.*"

"*Ja*, you told me that." *But I don't want to be-*

lieve it. That was her problem, not his, and she needed a way to deal with her ridiculous heart which kept believing Daniel would change his dreams to make hers come true.

He cleared his throat, as uncomfortable with the turn the conversation had taken as she was. "I've got something for Shelby." He opened one of the cupboard doors and pulled out a piece of wood about a foot long and eight inches wide. It'd been smoothed and polished, glinting beneath the skylight. "I spoke to Keely about this, because it might help Shelby with her occupational therapy." He held it out.

Hannah took it. Her eyes widened as she examined it. Into the board were set a variety of large wooden pegs and screws. Each had been painted a bright color. The pegs had been glued into place, so no amount of hammering would push them through the wood. The screws had been inserted so they could turn a few times, but couldn't be removed.

"What is it?" she asked.

"A toy that doubles as a therapy tool. Keely wanted Shelby to have some small objects to grip, and the pegs are the right size." He tapped one of the screws. "Turning these will strengthen Shelby's fingers and wrists."

She blinked back sudden tears. She wondered if she'd ever figure out Daniel. One minute, he was all business, talking about the company he wanted to establish and how he never would be a family man. The next, he was showing the depth of his heart by planning to give the beautiful house to his brother and by making such a *wunderbaar* gift for Shelby.

"You give it to her," Hannah choked out, so overwhelmed she could hardly speak. "Then she'll know it's from you."

Daniel called the toddler over to him. Setting the board on the floor, he said, "This is for you, *liebling.*"

"Da-dan!" cried Shelby in delight as she dropped with a plop to sit on the floor. Tossing Buzz-buzz aside, she reached for the red peg. Her fingers closed in front of it, but instead of getting frustrated as she often was during her therapy sessions, she tried again.

And again and again.

Hannah lost count of the number of times the little girl tried to grab the peg. She watched, holding her breath. When Shelby grasped the peg and chortled her deep laugh, Hannah clapped her hands and cheered.

Daniel came to his feet while Shelby tried to grasp the blue peg and was successful on her first try.

Through happy tears racing down her face, Hannah said, *"Danki,* Daniel!"

"I'm glad it makes you happy." His hand curved along her face, his thumb brushing away her tears.

She gazed at him, unable to speak as his arm slid around her waist, drawing her to him. He ran his fingers along her cheek, and she feared her trembling legs would forget how to hold her. She wanted to forget everything except for the yearning in his eyes. He whispered her name in the moment before his lips captured hers. When he tugged her to him, she curved her arms around his shoulders. Her hands clenched on his wool coat that couldn't disguise the work-hardened muscles beneath it.

Slowly he lifted his mouth from hers after grazing her lips with another swift kiss. His blue eyes glowed like a calm pond, but there was nothing serene about them. Emotions collided within them, and she couldn't help wondering if he was feeling the same joy she was. She hoped so because this moment was everything she'd dreamed of.

Before...

Hannah gasped and stepped away. Now wasn't before, and she'd learned something in the past three years about letting her heart lead the way. She seized Shelby who yelped a protest as her new toy clattered against the floor.

"*Danki* for showing us your house, Daniel, but we have to go."

He frowned. "Are you going to run away every time you let me a little bit past the walls you've raised to keep me away?"

"It's better I leave than wait for you to go without saying goodbye." The bitter words spilled from her mouth, erasing the pleasure she'd found in his kiss.

He flinched as if she'd struck him.

"I'm sorry," she whispered, cuddling Shelby close. "I shouldn't have said that."

"No." He stuffed his hands into his coat pockets and looked bleak. "You have every right to say that, because it's true. I messed up three years ago."

She took one step away, then another. He watched her until she reached the door. Bending, he picked up the toy he'd made for Shelby. He handed it and Buzz-buzz to Hannah. She thanked him and waited for him to say something.

But he didn't.

Neither did she as she opened the door and left. She hurried across the clearing and hoped he'd call her back.

But he didn't.

How foolish she'd been to kiss him! She'd dared to believe he'd come to love her as much as she'd loved him for so long.

But he didn't.

Chapter Thirteen

Hannah dropped a canning jar. It broke into a half dozen pieces, sliding across the bare floor. Leaving the shards where they were, she set Shelby in her high chair before her little sister could touch the broken glass. Hannah selected an apple oatmeal muffin from the ones cooling on the counter. Checking it wasn't too hot, she peeled off the paper and set the sweet muffin on the tray. The little girl took a big bite, scattering crumbs down the front of her.

Going to the laundry room, Hannah got the broom and dustpan. She began to sweep up the broken glass.

"That's the fourth thing you've broken since the quilting frolic," *Grossmammi* Ella said as she came into the kitchen. Counting on her fingers, she said, "A cup, a glass, the sugar bowl and the canning jar."

"I'll be more careful," she said like an obedient *kind*. It was easier to agree because she didn't have to think about it. She didn't want to think about anything when too many of her thoughts led to Daniel.

"Sit," her great-grandmother said, pointing to the table.

"I need to—"

"Shelby is in the high chair, and you and I have enough *gut* sense to step around the glass. Sit."

Hannah obeyed. Again it was easier than explaining she had too many chores to do this morning to sit and be scolded for being clumsy.

As soon as she sat across from her great-grandmother, *Grossmammi* Ella said, "I know I miss a lot, Hannah, and I'm sure I've forgotten more, but there are some things I can see. You're attracted to your Daniel."

Don't call him my *Daniel!* She silenced the thought which sounded petulant even in her head.

"*Grossmammi* Ella, you know I made a mistake trusting Daniel Stoltzfus once," she said. "I'd be a fool to do so again."

"Bah!" Her great-grandmother waved aside her words as if they were annoying gnats. "So you made a mistake? What was it? Two years ago?"

"Three."

"So you made a mistake three years ago. Everyone makes mistakes. The important thing is to learn from them. Learn what you did wrong and learn how with God's help, you can avoid the mistake again."

Hannah sighed. "So much easier said than done. I've been asking God to guide me in what I should do. I need to make sure I listen to Him instead of anyone else."

"Like the *gut*-looking young man who glows with joy when he visits?" *Grossmammi* Ella folded her thin arms on the table. "Your Daniel has the look my Earney had when he came to court me. And I see the happiness in your eyes when Daniel is at our door. It's like what I felt in my heart when Earney smiled at me. I tell you, Hannah, he's a *gut* man."

"*Ja, Grossdawdi* was—"

"Not my Earney. I'm talking about your Daniel. He's a *gut* man."

Looking away, she didn't want to admit she agreed. Daniel was a *gut* man, not the villain she'd created and nurtured in her imagination for the past three years. He was a hardworking man in pursuit of what he'd wanted.

The memory of Daniel's laugh rumbled through her head. His laugh—his real one, not the polite one he'd used when he first came to the house—was like the sound of distant thunder against the rolling hills. It resonated within her, slipping past the guard she'd put in place to keep her heart from being touched again. His joking had stripped away her anger.

"The *gut* Lord has given you three years to heal," her great-grandmother said, "and He has brought your Daniel back into your life. God has a reason for these things. If it's not to give you two a chance to reconsider, what else could it be?"

Hannah blinked on tears as her great-grandmother continued in a logical manner. This was the woman she remembered from fifteen years ago, before the Alzheimer's disease had begun to rob her of what she'd been.

Reaching across the table, Hannah cradled *Grossmammi* Ella's fragile hand. Her great-grandmother stretched to take Shelby's right hand while Hannah clasped her little sister's left. When her great-grandmother bowed her head in silent prayer, Hannah did the same, grateful for her family circle that was the perfect haven from the yearnings and fears in her heart.

Had anyone ever been as stupid as Daniel had been yesterday when he'd kissed Hannah? When he'd been walking out with her, he'd known better than to kiss her and let her think he was ready to offer her the future she wanted. He hadn't planned to kiss her yesterday either, but when he'd seen the joy on her face and knew he'd brought it to her, his longing to hold her had silenced his *gut* sense.

He glanced at her house through the rain which had returned at dawn. Hannah must know he was at the bridge. His crew had just gone home, leaving silence in their wake after a long day of cutting boards and nailing them in place. One more board needed to be cut; then Daniel could call it a day, too. The only sounds were the thud of the rain on the repaired roof and his conscience urging him to go to the Lambrights' house and apologize for what he'd done.

Which would be fine if he were sorry he'd kissed her. He wasn't. Not a bit. For years, he wondered if her lips would be as luscious and sweet as her honey, and he had his answer. They were. But instead of satisfying his curiosity and putting the idea of kissing her out of his head, the caress of her lips against his had whetted his longing for another kiss…and another…and another.

Irritated at his thoughts, he pounded the hammer against the board to wedge into the narrow curve so it would support that section of the arch. The hammer grazed his thumb. He yelped and dropped the hammer. Shaking his hand as if he could make the pain fall out, he surged to his feet.

He grimaced. He hadn't hit a finger since he was an apprentice learning how to wield a hammer. That was what he got for not paying attention to his work.

At a loud roar, Daniel looked up. A black sports car come to a stop by the barriers on the far end of the bridge. Its engine cut out, and the noise vanished. The door opened and out stepped a man with bright red hair and tattered blue jeans tucked into work boots that looked newer than Daniel's. He wore a leather jacket over a white shirt.

Coming to the concrete barrier, the *Englischer* waved.

"Can I help you?" Daniel called.

"You're Daniel Stoltzfus, right?" the *Englischer* asked in an odd accent Daniel had never heard.

"Ja." Hanging his hammer on his tool belt, he asked, "What can I do for you?"

"I was hoping to talk to you."

"Sure." Daniel walked with care on the thick stringers where the planks of the deck hadn't been secured into place. In the past two weeks, he'd had to traverse them often enough so he didn't have to watch every step he took, but he knew better than to get too overconfident. Not paying attention could lead to an accident far more serious than a throbbing thumb; then there wouldn't be any chance of finishing the bridge on time.

Stepping onto the asphalt, he strode to the barrier curving across the road from one set of guardrails to the other. He greeted the *Englischer* and waited for the man to state his business.

"I'm Liam O'Neill." The redhead hooked a thumb behind him toward the south. "I bought the McClellan farm near Strasburg. Do you know it?"

Daniel was intrigued by the lilt of the man's accent. "*Ja*, but not well."

"The barn and the house need work. Since my wife and I purchased the farm last month, I've been asking around for someone who could do the work. Your name has come up a lot. Would you be willing to stop by and take a look and see if you're interested in the project?"

"*Ja*, I'd be interested in seeing what you want done."

"We want what you're doing here." He gestured toward the bridge. "I've driven past a few times, and I like how you're updating the bridge without the changes being obvious. That's what my wife wants with the farmhouse. It's an old stone-end house like the one over there." He pointed to the Lambrights' house. "She wants what she calls a sympathetic renovation. Do you know what that is?"

"*Ja.* A house that lives like it's new and looks like it's old."

The *Englischer* grinned. "Exactly. When can you stop by?"

"With the rain, we're having to work whenever there's a break and plenty of light. How about tomorrow night around six?"

"Perfect." Liam offered his hand.

Daniel shook it as he said, "If you've got a list of projects you want done, that would help us get started."

"I'll have my wife pull her lists together into one." He chuckled, then turned to leave. He paused and said, "You know, you're the first Amish man I've ever spoken with."

"And you're the first I've ever spoken with from…"

"Ireland. Dublin."

That explained his accent and his name, and Daniel grinned. "So let's hope this project has no more firsts for either of us."

"By the way, will you need transportation?"

"My horse and buggy will be fine, but *danki.*" He added, "Thanks."

"I figured that out," Liam said. "Okay, it sounds as if we've got a plan for tomorrow night. You can look around and see what you think is possible and what isn't. I should warn you. My wife wants to open up the small rooms."

"You'll need a structural engineer to determine how best to support any load-bearing walls."

"I don't know any in the area."

"I know a *gut* one, and I'll be glad to give you his name and phone number whether you and I work together or not."

"That's generous of you, Mr. Stoltzfus."

"Call me Daniel. Plain folk don't put weight in titles."

Liam nodded and walked to his car. The engine awoke with another mighty growl.

Daniel watched it drive away. He'd had his dream handed to him after years of waiting and hoping and saving to buy the equipment he needed and making contacts in the construction business throughout Lancaster County. He'd just been offered a job where he could be the boss and work with the best artisans he knew.

His dream was coming true.

So why wasn't he excited?

He glanced again toward the Lambrights' house. Maybe he wasn't as thrilled as he'd expected because he didn't have anyone special to share the news with. But how could he bring Hannah into his life when he could see the long, long days and nights of work ahead if Liam hired him? Time he wouldn't be able to spend with her and her family. It wouldn't be right.

Or so he'd thought. All of the sudden, he wasn't too sure.

Of anything.

Daniel was halfway to Paradise Springs when he turned his buggy around and headed back toward Hannah's house. Why was he making himself miserable? Hannah had said several times she wanted to be his friend, and shouldn't he share his *gut* news with his *gut* friend? More than anyone else, she'd paid the price for his ambition. It seemed only right she should be the first one he told about the opportunity to make his dream come true.

Hoping he wasn't trying to fool himself again, he rode through the thickening twilight which had come earlier with the rain. He wasn't sure, but it seemed to be raining harder than it'd been earlier. Or maybe he was, like everyone else, tired of day after day of rain.

He heard the raised voices and Shelby's crying as he reached the door of the Lambrights' house. No, not raised *voices*. Just a single one even louder than the toddler's frantic cries. A woman's voice at a furious pitch. He opened the door and heard a hand slap hard against someone's skin.

As he watched in disbelief, Hannah recoiled away from her great-grandmother. Hannah was trying to reason with her, but *Grossmammi* Ella's eyes snapped with fury as the old woman raised her hand again. Beyond them, Shelby clung to a chair and her stuffed honeybee and sobbed.

Daniel stepped between Hannah and *Grossmammi* Ella who snarled at him to get out of the way so she could teach that horrible woman not to flirt with her husband. Gently he caught the elderly woman's birdlike wrist and lowered her arm to her side. When she cried out and tried to break free, he held her easily.

"Now, now," he said as if she were no older than Shelby, "you don't want to do that, *Grossmammi* Ella. You don't want to hurt Hannah."

"I wouldn't hurt Hannah," the old woman retorted. "But Mima needs to get her own husband."

"Mima?" he mouthed in Hannah's direction.

She replied, "Later." Out loud, she added, "*Grossmammi* Ella, let me get you a cup of chamomile tea. It'll make you feel better, ain't so?"

Daniel watched the old woman's face and saw it alter from rage to bewilderment. He released her wrist but kept his hand beneath her elbow as he steered her toward the chair by the living room window. Draping a quilt over her knees, he sighed. *Lost.* The word burst into his mind. *Grossmammi* Ella was lost.

Picking up Shelby, he soothed her by making faces and playing peekaboo. He kept at it while Hannah made tea and took it to her great-grandmother. Not once did she look in his direction, but he could see she was blushing. Why? She couldn't be embarrassed, could she, that he'd halted the old woman's rampage?

She was, he realized, when she wouldn't meet his eyes as she returned to the kitchen. He took her elbow, as he had *Grossmammi* Ella's, and urged her to come with him out onto the front porch. She paused long enough to collect her coat and Shelby's.

He closed the door behind them, so their voices wouldn't reach into the house. While she pulled on her coat, he slipped Shelby's arms into hers. He sat on the top step where the rain didn't reach, bouncing the little girl on his knee. When Hannah perched beside him, he ached to put his arm around her shoulders. He resisted, not wanting to do anything to upset her more.

"Are you okay?" he asked as she stared at the rushing creek across the road.

"*Ja. Danki* for helping."

"Does she get like this often?"

"Not often, but often enough." Her smile appeared and fled in a heartbeat. "Usually I can calm her, but sometimes I can't."

He was about to answer, but paused when he

realized the enormity of what she'd said. His voice cracked as he asked, "She's hit you before?"

Not meeting his gaze, she nodded. "I know she doesn't mean to hurt me. She gets mired in her memories."

"She could hurt you badly." He frowned. "She'd hit you the day you removed the bees from the bridge, hadn't she? That's why you kept your beekeeper's hat on as long as you could. Why did you let me think you fell?"

Flinging out her hands, she said, "Because I knew you'd react like this."

"Being angry that she hit you? Of course, I'm going to react like this." He caught one of her hands as he turned her face toward him. "Why didn't you tell me the truth?"

"I was honest with you."

"But you said—"

"I slipped on the wet grass and bumped against the bridge." Tears glistened in her luminous eyes. "It happened, Daniel, as I said. I told you the truth, but not all of it."

"The bruise was from your great-grandmother striking you." He didn't make it a question.

"Ja."

He pretended to recoil when Shelby bopped him on the chin with Buzz-buzz, but he didn't look away from Hannah. How could she be so calm? The Amish believed in nonresistance, he knew well, but that didn't mean she had to endure her great-grandmother's blows.

When he said as much, Hannah gave him a sad smile. "Daniel, you didn't get upset when Shelby hit you just now with her toy, did you?"

"She's not much more than a *boppli*. She doesn't know what she's doing."

"*Grossmammi* Ella is the same. She doesn't know what she's doing. So how can I get mad at *Grossmammi* Ella if I don't get mad at Shelby?"

He opened his mouth to reply; then he realized he didn't have anything to say. Hannah was right. With each passing day, her great-grandmother's mind was wandering further and further into the past. The sudden shifts in mood from happy to furious and frustrated no longer startled him as much as they had at the beginning.

"But you can't have her here with you if she's going to hurt you and Shelby," he said.

"She hasn't raised her hand to Shelby."

"Not yet."

"She won't. Each time she's hit me, she's believed I was someone else, someone who was trying to keep her from her beloved Earney. If she knew me, she never would have swung her hand. She's scared of what she can't remember and uncertain of what she can."

"But if she thinks Shelby is someone else…"

"When she's confused, she thinks Shelby is

me. She'd never hurt a toddler." She took his hand, startling him. "Daniel, she's my family. Until Shelby came, she was my only family. I can't turn my back on her because it's not easy to take care of her. She took care of me during times when I'm sure I wasn't easy to be around."

"She never struck you, though."

Putting her fingers to her cheek, she said, "Each time, the bruise heals. My heart wouldn't heal if I put her into some sort of nursing home. I need you to understand."

"I do understand," he replied as he tried to imagine having to make that same choice for his *mamm*. "You should seek Reuben's advice."

"I have." She met his gaze. "He urged me to do two things. One was to love my great-grandmother, even if I despise her condition. The other was to remember none of us is alone if we trust God is with us. Knowing that has gotten me through the toughest times so I can enjoy the happy ones. I know it won't be long until she's called home, and I don't want to miss a minute we've got together."

When tears fell down her cheeks, he tilted her head on his shoulder and held her without saying anything else. He didn't want to let her go. Not ever.

He looked over her head toward the bridge where he'd been offered a chance to make his dreams come true. Could he be the man Hannah needed? Until he knew the answer, he mustn't say anything else either.

Chapter Fourteen

When a knock came just as Hannah was about to turn off the propane light in the kitchen, she stiffened. Who was calling at this late hour?

Her wish that Daniel was at the door was absurd. There wasn't any reason for him to come from the far side of Paradise Springs at this hour, but she missed him holding her as he had earlier when he comforted her.

It'd been a tough day. Her great-grandmother had been on edge until she went to bed right after supper. She hadn't lost her temper again, but each time Shelby made a sound, the old woman flinched and glared in the *kind*'s direction.

Had Daniel been right? Would the time come when *Grossmammi* Ella was a danger to the toddler?

The thought added another layer of pain to Hannah's headache that had plagued her since her great-grandmother struck her. She hoped a *gut* night's sleep would ease the ache, and she would wake up feeling well.

But first she needed to see who was knocking. She didn't want either Shelby or *Grossmammi* Ella to be routed up, because it might take a long time to get them back to sleep.

Opening the door, Hannah gasped when she saw Chief McMurray standing on her porch. Why was he there?

"May I come in?" he asked, his face giving no clue to his thoughts.

Her legs were stiff as she backed away to let him in. He took off his cap with its insignia. She wasn't sure if she should offer to take it or not. She led the way into the living room and motioned for him to sit.

He did on the sofa and, as soon as she was perched on her great-grandmother's favorite chair, he said, "There's no way to say this gently. Hannah, your father and his wife were killed in a highway accident last night."

"Oh…" She should feel something. Sorrow, regret, anger…something, but she'd become numb. Maybe her feelings had been burned away already after the horrible day. But it was her *daed* the chief of police was talking about. She should feel something.

"The state police in Nebraska contacted me."

"My *daed* was in Nebraska?" She couldn't guess why he'd been so far away.

"Yes, and the state police told me that there had been a sudden snow squall on the highway last night. A complete whiteout. A couple of big semis skidded and caused a chain reaction."

"Was one of them my *daed*'s?" She'd guessed he was a truck driver from the multiple places he'd sent postcards from, but she'd never been sure.

"He wasn't driving either of the ones that caused the accident, but your father's rig was caught in it." He leaned forward, and his kind gaze caught and held hers as he added, "Hannah, you need to know something important. The officer I spoke with said witnesses told him that your father swerved to miss a school bus and a couple of SUVs. If he hadn't turned to avoid them, his truck wouldn't have rolled as it did. But, by doing so, he saved those peoples' lives."

She knew Chief McMurray expected her to be proud of her *daed*, but the numbness smothered her. "*Danki* for coming to tell me," she whispered.

"Is there someone I can contact for you?"

Daniel, her heart cried, but she said, "If you'll let the bishop know, I'd appreciate it."

"I will." Coming to his feet, he added, "I'm sorry for your loss, Hannah."

She thanked him again, but didn't add she'd lost her *daed* over fifteen years before. What had been lost tonight was her dream of seeing him again and discovering why he'd abandoned her and Shelby. The chance to learn the truth was gone forever.

Daniel frowned when he walked toward Hannah's house the next morning. It was the day the occupational therapist came to work with Shelby. The sessions with Keely were in the morning when the toddler was most alert and amiable to play "the games" the therapist had devised to help her.

But the road in front of the Lambrights' house was empty. Keely's black pickup wasn't in the driveway either. Curiosity propelled him toward the house, not only to discover why the therapist hadn't come but to learn how Hannah fared in the wake of yesterday's uproar.

When the front door opened and *Grossmammi* Ella stood there, he was so startled that he mumbled his greeting.

"What are you doing here?" she asked as if he were a naughty *kind*.

He had no idea how to answer the old woman's question. Was she in the present day or had her mind wandered again into the past? Had she tried to hit Hannah again?

"I come to work with Shelby and Keely at this time."

Grossmammi Ella's nose wrinkled. "That *Englisch* woman has many squirrelly ideas." Her answer told him she was aware of what was currently going on.

"She's trying to help Shelby." He glanced around the room. "Where's Shelby? Did she and Hannah go somewhere?" He couldn't imagine anything that would compel Hannah to leave her great-grandmother alone.

As if he'd said that aloud, an elderly man strode in from the kitchen. He was almost bald and had a round, cheerful face. His clothes and thick black mustache identified him as an *Englischer*.

"Hi! I'm Barry Jones."

Daniel introduced himself and glanced from the old man to Hannah's great-grandmother. "So you're here to keep *Grossmammi* Ella company?" he asked, not wanting to insult the elderly woman.

"Yep. We've been talking about how soon we can plant our gardens," Barry replied. "Do you garden, young man?"

"No. I'm a carpenter."

"The one working on our covered bridge?"

"Ja." Hoping he didn't seem rude, he asked, "Where are Hannah and Shelby?"

Instead of answering his question, *Grossmammi* Ella wagged a finger under his nose. "Why are you here? You should be with Hannah. She needs someone with her, and she wouldn't let me go with her."

"Where?"

"Into the village. She's seeing some *Englisch* lawyer." *Grossmammi* Ella's mouth twisted with distaste. "Trust my foolish grandson to do something else stupid. Not only did he jump the fence and leave his daughter behind without a second thought, but he shared his business with an *Englischer*. That's not our way." She glanced at Barry, who shrugged at her words.

Daniel didn't argue with the elderly woman either, though he knew many Amish folks sought out the help and advice of an attorney with business or family matters, especially with incorporation of businesses or probate issues.

"Hannah's *daed* has contacted her?" he asked.

Barry answered after glancing at the old woman, who'd turned and walked toward her chair, "Isaac and his wife were killed in an accident in Nebraska. The police came to let the family know last night." He glanced at *Grossmammi* Ella. "I'm not sure if she comprehends the news yet."

Weight pressed onto Daniel's chest, making it impossible to breathe. Hannah's *daed* was dead? Suddenly he couldn't think of anything other than finding Hannah and comforting her, but he somehow managed to ask, "Do you know which attorney she's seeing?"

"Some peculiar *Englisch* name," *Grossmammi* Ella said as she sat in her favorite chair. "How can I be expected to remember it?"

"Didn't you say it was on the letter delivered to Hannah this morning, Ella?" asked her neighbor.

"Ja." She frowned at Daniel. "I suppose you want to see it."

"I'd like to, if you don't mind." He chafed at the delay. Hannah shouldn't be alone after receiving such news.

She made a sniffing sound as if he'd made an impertinent reply. "It's on the table in the kitchen."

Daniel half-ran to get the white envelope. He glanced at the return address and smiled when he saw the Marianelli and Loggins logo. Quentin Marianelli handled legal matters for many plain families around Paradise Springs. Daniel should have guessed Isaac Lambright had used his services.

"What are you waiting for?" Hannah's great-grandmother asked. "She shouldn't have gone alone. You should be there with her."

Daniel agreed. He spun on his heel, crossed the room and yanked the door open. Calling a goodbye over his shoulder, he crossed the porch in a single step and then jumped onto the grass. His feet almost slid out from beneath him, but he regained his balance and climbed into his buggy that he'd left by the bridge. He shouted to the men working there to let them know he'd be back when he could. He didn't wait for their response.

As soon as he arrived at the lawyer's office in a pleasant house along Route 30 in the heart of Paradise Springs, Daniel saw Hannah sitting stiffly with Shelby on her lap. Her eyes widened as he entered, and he saw her relief she wasn't alone. As she'd been too long because he'd walked away.

Taking a chair beside her, he said, "Your great-grandmother told me where you'd gone, and I thought you'd like some company."

"Ja," she said in a whisper.

He started to tell her how sorry he was about her *daed*, but a man in a dark suit came over to where they were sitting.

"Hannah Lambright?" When she nodded, he said, "I'm Quentin Marianelli. Thank you for coming today. I'm sorry for your loss."

"Danki," she replied. "This is my little sister, Shelby, and Daniel Stoltzfus."

The attorney greeted them before asking them to come with him to his office.

"Do you want me to come?" he asked when Hannah stood.

"Ja." She didn't add anything else.

He followed her and the lawyer down a short hall to an office dominated by a large desk and a wall of bookshelves. The attorney sat behind the desk and motioned for them to take the two chairs in front of it.

"I'm glad you're here, Daniel," the lawyer said as soon as they were settled in their places. "You can help us with one procedural step before we can proceed. I know you don't carry identification, so will you vouch this woman is, indeed, Hannah Lambright, a woman you have known for…?"

"Almost five years," Daniel supplied.

"A woman you have known for over four years," the attorney said as he scribbled on the form waiting on his desk. "Do you vouch for her identity?" He gave them a brief smile. "All you need to do, Daniel, is say yes or no."

"Ja. I mean, yes."

"Either works fine." Scrawling something across the bottom of the page, he pushed the page toward Daniel. "Will you sign at the bottom, too? By signing, you're acknowledging your statement about Hannah is the truth."

What had he said? That he'd known her for years. True, but there were depths to Hannah he hadn't realized existed until the past few weeks. She was a woman who stood strong against the storms of life and, despite what she'd experienced—or maybe *because* of it—she offered every bit of her strength to others as she held them up to God in action and in prayer. He wondered if he'd ever met another person who so embodied God's grace, giving everything she had and expecting nothing in return.

The attorney slipped the paper into a folder, then looked again at Hannah. "Do you wish the rest of our conversation to be private?"

"Having Daniel here is fine." Her voice was so dull she sounded as if a large part of her had died along with her *daed*.

"All right." Opening the folder, he said, "Your father left detailed instructions for his funeral." He looked uncomfortable as he went on, "He did not want his remains to be brought to Paradise Springs. He wanted to be buried in Michigan where he lived when he wasn't on the road. He told me he found it too painful even to think of returning here after your mother died."

Daniel looked at the toddler who was wiggling on Hannah's lap. Isaac had returned long enough to leave Shelby on the porch.

"Usually we wait until after the funeral to read the will," the attorney said.

"My *daed* had a will?" Hannah asked as she set Shelby on the floor.

"Yes." Mr. Marianelli tapped the folder. "He prepared it after your mother died and left it with me. It's straightforward with his estate divided between his children. There is some insurance money, and we'll deal with that when the funds are disbursed." He tapped the folder on the desk. "Why I wanted you to come here today was I received two letters from your father. He wanted you to have them after his death. He gave the first one to me about three years ago."

"He was here three years ago?" Betrayal rang through her question.

"Yes," said the attorney. "He was pleased you were making yourself a future with a good man, Hannah. Those were his exact words. He didn't want to do anything to ruin your happiness with your young man."

Sickness clawed at Daniel's gut. Three years ago, Hannah had been walking out with him. Isaac must have chanced to see them together or heard they were courting. Because he was under the *bann*, Isaac had assumed speaking with his daughter might cause trouble between her and her admirer.

Hannah reached over and took his hand as she had on the porch yesterday. Only yesterday?

It seemed like a lifetime ago. He squeezed her hand, not surprised she was offering *him* comfort.

Mr. Marianelli took an unmarked envelope from the file and held it out.

Daniel held his breath as he saw the last remnants of color fall away from her face as she stared at the letter that contained the final words her *daed* would ever have for her.

As she stared at the envelope, Hannah wanted to flee, but she must read what her *daed* had wanted her to read, for herself and for Shelby. She was grateful Daniel had arrived before she was called in to talk with the attorney. She'd wanted Daniel to stay because too much of the conversations around her sounded like Shelby's gibberish.

Her fingers trembled as she reached for the envelope. "Should I read it now?"

"If you don't mind," the lawyer said.

When Daniel put a steadying hand on her arm, she didn't glance at him. She opened the envelope and lifted out a single folded page. She opened it.

Her *daed* had printed the four lines, but the letters were smudged as if he'd erased some words several times. She began reading aloud,

"Dearest Hannah,

"Forgive me. I can't stay. Each time I see you, I see your *mamm*. I am weak, I know, but you'll have a better life without me.

"Your *Daed*"

That was it. *Daed* had left because he couldn't bear to look at her because she reminded him too much of her *mamm*. How ironic Shelby had been fearful of her at first because everyone said Hannah had grown to resemble him.

"That's all it says." She folded the page and put it into its envelope. She placed it on Mr. Marianelli's desk.

The attorney shuffled pages in the file, then drew out another envelope. It had printing in the upper left-hand corner. When he handed it to Hannah, he said, "This arrived a few weeks ago. On the back, you can see the date it was delivered."

She turned over the envelope imprinted with the name of a hotel chain. With a gasp, she stared at the date. "It's two days after Shelby was left at our house."

She ripped the envelope getting it open and pulled out another sheet with writing on both sides. Seeing her name on the top on one side, she began reading,

"Dearest Hannah,

"You must have many questions after finding a little girl on the front porch of *Grossmammi* Ella's house, but I have space to answer only the important ones. Shelby is your little sister. Karen tells me she's actually your half-sister. That's Shelby's *mamm*. Karen. She and I know a special child like Shelby needs a stable home, and we can't give her that. She shouldn't be living in a big rig. She needs extra help, and she needs someone she can depend on to get her help. That's you, Hannah. We would have kept her with us awhile longer, but a new job has come up in Alaska, and we're going to head that way once we've finished the other jobs we have scheduled. It's a good job, and it pays well. I'll send money to you and Shelby when I can. I should have sent you money before, but somehow the rig always needed repairs or times were lean. I could afford to send postcards, and I hope you thought of me when you received them and knew I was thinking of you.

"I know you think I'm abandoning Shelby as I did you, but no matter how much distance has separated us, nothing could remove you from my heart, Hannah. Your *mamm* and I loved you. I still love you, and

I miss you, just as I'll miss Shelby. But I thank God my daughters will be safe with each other.

"Your *Daed*"

No one spoke as Hannah lowered the letter to her lap. Her *daed* loved her. The pain she'd expected when told her *daed* had died rushed over her like a fierce storm. She'd never hear him say those words again.

"May I take this with me?" she asked, struggling to hold in the tears stinging her eyes.

Mr. Marianelli smiled sadly. "Of course. The letters are yours. I want you to know there's no hurry to go over your father's last will and testament. We can arrange a meeting in a week or two at a time convenient for you."

Coming to her feet, she thanked him as she put the letters in her bag. She went to where Shelby had been paging through magazines, looking for pictures. Several were scattered on the floor by the table. Putting them back, she picked up the toddler. She went with Daniel from the office and to where his buggy was parked beside hers.

So many thoughts were ricocheting through her mind she was surprised her head could hold them. Everything she'd come to believe had been turned upside down. She wasn't unlovable. Her *daed* loved her as did her great-grandmother and her adorable little sister. No half about it. Shelby was her sister.

"Hannah?" asked Daniel as she put Shelby in the buggy. "Do you want me to go back to the house with you?"

She shook her head. "No, I need time to think about this and to share it with *Grossmammi* Ella."

"Are you sure? I know this has to be tough for you."

"It is."

"Isn't there anything I can do to help?"

Climbing into her buggy, she shook her head. "I appreciate your offer, Daniel, but the truth is I can manage with God's help." She looked into his handsome face, fighting her fingers that wanted to push the ebony hair from his brow. "*Danki* for being here today. I know you've got to get going to meet with a potential client."

He stared at her in disbelief. "How did you hear that?"

"The *Englischer* who is looking to hire you heard about you from our neighbor, Barry Jones. Barry told *Grossmammi* Ella, and I saw you talking to a stranger at the bridge yesterday. I put one and one together." It took all her strength to smile. "I'm happy for you, Daniel. It's what you've wanted for so long."

"I meant to tell you, but I couldn't when you

were upset. I could come over to your house after—"

"I don't think you should come by as often as you have."

His dark brows lowered as he frowned. "You mean you don't want me to help with Shelby's therapy?"

"You're going to make me say it, aren't you?"

"Say what?"

She forced herself to meet his eyes. What she had to say was going to be hurtful, but it had to be better to say it than to be heartbroken again. "I don't want to think I can depend on you, Daniel, and then realize I can't."

"You can depend on me." He frowned, his brows knitting together. "Haven't I been here to help you?"

"*Ja*, you have been. But you've got a chance to have the work you've been waiting for. I'm afraid it will be like before when—"

Realization of what she was trying not to say must have hit him because the color washed from his face. He looked as horrified as if she'd told him to jump off the bridge.

"I've told you I'm not that man any longer," he said.

"I know."

"But you can't believe me."

Her heart cramped when he didn't make it a

question. "I want to, but I believed you before. I can't risk that again, so you should focus on your new job instead of us."

"By us, you mean you, don't you?"

"I mean me, and I mean us. I don't want Shelby to believe you'll be there for her and then have your job keep you from coming to see her as you've promised." She looked from him to her little sister who was yawning and cuddling her stuffed honeybee. "Really, Daniel, I'm glad this opportunity has come along for you. I want you to be happy."

He opened his mouth, then shut it. Swallowing hard, he squared his shoulders. "Can I come and see Shelby?"

"Of course. She likes to do her therapy games with you." Every instinct urged her to put her hand on his arm to comfort him. She didn't. As he turned away, she added, "Daniel?"

"What?"

"I'm sorry."

As he got into his buggy, she thought she heard him say, "I am, too." Then he was gone.

And her heart broke again. Her efforts to protect it had been for nothing as she realized the one truth she'd tried to ignore: she'd fallen in love with him again as hard and deeply as the first time. Only this time she'd pushed him away before he could do the same to her.

She put her hands over her face as sobs ripped through her.

A tiny hand patted her cheek. She looked into Shelby's dark eyes.

"Han-han," the little girl murmured, throwing her arms around Hannah's neck and burying her face against her shoulder.

Hannah wrapped her arms around the little girl. Shelby had never spoken her name before, and the *kind*'s message was clear. She didn't want Hannah to cry. Holding the toddler close, Hannah wept for everything she'd lost and everything she'd found…and everything she'd lost again.

Chapter Fifteen

The rain had been falling hard all night, and it'd become heavier as Daniel pulled into the parking lot for the Stoltzfus Family Shops. If he were the fanciful type, he would have said the weather reflected his bleak state of mind.

Puddles, poked by raindrops, marked lower spots in front of the shops. He didn't have to steer Taffy around them. The horse hated puddles, so he maneuvered the buggy without guidance from Daniel. Just as well, because Daniel's attention wasn't on driving.

The parking lot was deserted. Nobody, not even *Englischers* in their cars, wanted to be out on such a miserable day. He wouldn't be out himself if he didn't want to get advice from his brothers.

Every prayer he'd sent up in the long hours since he'd last spoken with Hannah had led him to the truth. He needed help. He'd been trying to figure out his uneven relationship with Hannah by himself for too long…and failing.

He'd known she'd find out about the possible job with Liam O'Neill sooner or later. He'd been going to tell her himself before the appalling scene with her great-grandmother and then the news of her *daed*'s tragic death. Not once had he imagined she'd congratulate him on the job and then tell him it'd be better if they didn't see each other so often.

Parking in front of Joshua's buggy shop, he jumped out and bent his head as the rain pelted him like a hundred tiny needles. He hurried onto the covered area in front of the shops and shook water off his straw hat and shoulders. He walked into the vast room that was filled to overflowing with equipment and buggy parts on the other side of a half wall. Five of Daniel's six brothers were there. His oldest brother, Joshua, had brewed *kaffi*, and Amos had brought some cookies and muffins from the grocery store. Isaiah's hands were ingrained with black soot from his work in the smithy behind the shops, but he held a chocolate chip cookie with a big bite out of it. Jeremiah sat to one side, rubbing varnish into a small box he must have been working on before he came to Joshua's shop. Joining them was Ezra, who soon would be so busy with spring chores he wouldn't have time for enjoying a cup of *kaffi* with his brothers.

They all looked toward the door as Daniel entered. He saw the glances they exchanged before putting on innocent expressions. They'd been talking about him. Had word already gone through the Amish grapevine about Hannah dumping him yesterday?

"Kaffi?" asked Joshua with a strained smile.

"Getting something to warm me after that cold rain sounds like a *gut* idea," he replied, following his oldest brother's lead of pretending as if everything was normal.

Daniel took the steaming cup. All the chairs had been claimed, so he sat on the half wall dividing the shop. Holding the cup to his face, he appreciated the heat billowing from it.

"The rain is going to turn to sleet or snow if it gets much colder," he said after taking a sip.

"We had enough snow already during the winter." Ezra gave an emoted shudder. "I didn't think it'd ever stop."

"It did when it turned to rain."

His brothers chuckled, and Daniel relaxed. He liked making his brothers laugh, and having them do so made the tension tightening his shoulders ease.

"Where's Micah?" he asked as he took a cookie from the plate Joshua held out to him.

Among the cookies from the grocery store, he saw a few of the delicious date-nut cookies his oldest brother's wife, Rebekah, baked. With a cockeyed grin, he snatched two of those before Joshua offered the plate to the others.

"He said something about taking *Mamm* out to Reuben's house." Amos winked at him. "I'm not sure why *Mamm* decided she needed to go on such a lousy day, but it's easy to guess why Micah was eager to take her."

"Unless he's willing to talk to Katie Kay, there's no reason for him to go," Daniel said.

Joshua began, "His spirit is willing—"

"But his courage is weak," said Ezra with a chuckle.

"I seem to remember," Jeremiah said as he looked up, "how we had to intervene for you and Leah when your courage was weak, Ezra."

The brothers hooted with laughter.

"How's the work coming at the bridge?" asked Amos.

"It'd go better if the rain would stop," Daniel replied and took another bite of a cookie. He knew what was on his brothers' minds. How long before they asked about Hannah?

Ezra chuckled, but with little humor. "The same thing I said about getting the corn in the field. As wet as it is, though I could get the planting started with my team, the seed will rot before it has a chance to grow."

"If we could get two days without rain, we'd be finished out at the bridge."

"I hear you're taking a job with an *Englischer* in Strasburg next." Isaiah held out his cup for a refill.

Tilting the pot over it, Daniel said, "It's not for sure. And don't call Liam O'Neill an *Englischer*. When I went over to talk to him about his project, he told me that it's an insult to *gut* Irishmen everywhere to be labeled *Englisch*." He kept his tone light because he didn't want anyone to know how hard it'd been for him to have that meeting after his strained conversation with Hannah outside the attorney's office.

It'd taken all his determination to be able to act as if he only cared about helping Liam and his wife renovate the old farmhouse that was close to falling in. He'd answered their questions and proposed an idea or two to make the project work, but his thoughts had constantly veered to Hannah. How could he fault her for trying to protect herself and her family after how he'd treated her? He should be grateful she hadn't spoken of how her *daed* might have sought her out if Isaac hadn't believed her future was set with Daniel. That thought shadowed him, making sleep impossible.

Joshua didn't look at him. "Once you're done at the bridge, you won't have many chances to spend time with Hannah, ain't so?"

"Ja." So much for his appearance of not having a care in the world. He should have known he couldn't fool his older brothers.

"Unless you ask her to walk out with you," Isaiah said.

"Not likely. I ruined everything last time with her." *And this time.*

"You did," Joshua said as his other brothers nodded. "I have to admit I was surprised she wanted anything to do with you once she removed the bees from the bridge."

"I don't know if she would have if it hadn't been for Shelby. The *kind* preferred me at first."

"You know what the *Englischers* say, don't you?" asked Ezra as he reached for another chocolate chip cookie.

"What's that?" he asked, though the twinkle in his brother's eye warned he wouldn't like hearing what Ezra had to say.

"There's no accounting for taste." Ezra's retort brought more howls of laughter from his brothers.

Daniel accepted the teasing with a wry grin. The Stoltzfus brothers ribbed one another, but also stood behind one another in trying times. They'd come together to support their *mamm* and each other when *Daed* died, and they'd done the same when two of the brothers had lost their wives. Joshua was married again, and Daniel hoped Isaiah would eventually as well.

"Speaking of Hannah," he said, "let me ask you a question."

Again his brothers exchanged a glance. He wished he understood what they were signaling to each other, but, for once, he wasn't part of the silent discussion.

"Go ahead." Amos leaned forward, clasping his hands between his knees.

He did, before he lost his nerve. "I've been wondering how you do it. Except for Jeremiah, Micah and me, you've been married or are getting married. What's the secret to owning a business and having a wife and a family? How do you have everything at the same time?"

"You're kidding, ain't so?" asked Joshua.

Ezra shook his head. "It's impossible to do everything. Have a wife, have a family, have a job."

"But you do it!" Daniel exclaimed.

"*Ja*, we do it." Ezra sighed. "We do it, but no matter how hard we try, something or someone gets too little attention."

"It's like trying to roll a log," added Joshua. "You have to adjust to keep from falling in the water, and sometimes, no matter how hard you try, you get dunked."

"Only you can decide what's your priority." Isaiah sighed, a sure sign the conversation wasn't easy for him because his beloved Rose had died less than a year before. "And then, there are times when you have no hope of keeping things in balance. Something has to give."

Daniel ate the cookies and two more as he listened to his brothers talk about the occasions when their jobs had intruded on their family time and other times when family had to take a back seat to their work obligations. His spirits fell lower and lower. Before he got depressed, he stood and thanked his brothers for their advice.

As he went outside, he heard his name from behind him. Amos walked out of the shop and clapped him on the shoulder. Together they stood on the covered porch and stared at the rain.

"You can't say when love is going to come into your life." Amos shrugged, then sighed. "Look at me! I didn't expect to fall in love when I decided to halt a miniature thief before Christmas. Now *Mamm* and Belinda are discussing wedding plans, though we won't be married until October or November."

"But you were smart enough to hold on to love once you had it."

"After learning the hard way that you need to be sure it's truly love. If you want my advice, Daniel, here it is. Once you know it's love, don't let it go. You've been blessed with a second chance to accept God's most precious gift. You blew it once. Why would you risk doing so again? You may never have a third chance."

"But, after listening to you, I don't know how I can keep everything in balance."

"You can't. Not by yourself. You have to bring God into it, Daniel. Hand over the things to Him that you can't do by yourself. Not that he's going to borrow a hammer and work beside you."

"I wasn't expecting that!" He chuckled, glad his older brother was being honest with him.

Amos didn't smile as he put his hand on Daniel's shoulder again and looked him square in the eyes. "What God can do for you, if you'll let Him, is reach into you and lift the weight of your obligations from your heart. The obligations will still be there, but you'll know no matter what happens, you never have to handle them alone. Going to God should be your first choice, Daniel, not your last resort."

Daniel stared at him as the words struck a chord deep within him. Hannah had said much the same thing, but he'd thought what worked for her wouldn't work for him. God had more important things to do than listen to Daniel go on and on about his dreams.

Didn't He?

"Think about it," Amos said before walking

away as a car pulled into the lot and parked in front of his shop. He waved to the two women scurrying through the rain. He held the door open for them, then followed them into the store.

As Daniel climbed into his buggy and turned Taffy along the road leading toward the covered bridge, he couldn't think of anything but Amos's advice. Go to God first with his problems?

Is that what I should do, Father? As he asked the question, he heard the answer in his heart. Who had Daniel gone to with his worries as a child? To his *daed*, who helped him find a way to ease his concerns and solve his problems. Why hadn't Daniel considered before that his relationship with his heavenly Father should be the same as with his *daed*?

By the time he reached the covered bridge, Daniel's head hurt with the thoughts rushing through it. He had a lot to sort out while he worked on nailing the last remaining boards into place on the deck. Once the rain eased, he and his crew could finish the sides of the bridge and paint them. After that, he could start the work at the O'Neills', and he'd have no excuse to come to the creek.

He glanced along it toward Hannah's house. Nobody was visible there, which was no surprise with the clatter of rain on the buggy's roof. He looked away, knowing he needed to figure out a lot before he tried to insert himself into the lives of Hannah and her family again.

Stopping the buggy by the bridge, he apologized to Taffy for leaving the horse out in the rain. He could take the horse to Hannah's barn, but he wasn't ready to face her.

He walked into the bridge and found it deserted. He'd told his crew not to bother to come if the rain continued today because they needed a dry day to work on the exterior. Moving to the far end, he stood by the thick board that was ready to be put into place.

Daniel bit back a gasp as he looked down. Hunter's Mill Creek had risen so high it was a foot or less from the bottom of the bridge. It had swallowed large sections of its banks and was crawling toward the road. Lost in his thoughts while he drove to the bridge, he'd missed how high and fast the creek was running.

Leaving the shelter of the covered bridge and walking out into the storm, Daniel ducked his head. The wind blew rain hard into his face, and he pulled up the collar of his work coat to protect his cheeks. The rain was falling faster by the minute. It was as if someone had turned on a faucet in the sky and left it running. None of the previous storms had been this bad.

He leaned out over the abutment and watched the water race under the bridge. The current of

the usually sleepy creek was so swift that foam
was splashing into the air whenever the water hit
a submerged stone. Branches and other debris
rushed past, disappearing beneath the water and
then reappearing farther downstream.

Would the bridge hold?

He climbed over the guardrail and balanced a
moment on the top of the stone abutment. Sliding on his feet and hands down the steep hill,
he took care to go slow. If he tumbled into the
creek, he might not get out alive. He braced his
feet on the hillside and held his hand to his forehead. That kept the rain from his eyes while he
appraised the work he and his crew had done
over the past month.

The braces along the arch connecting one side
of the bridge support to the other remained in
place. The rotted boards had been replaced beneath the trusses and along the roadbed. Wind-
driven raindrops splattered against the arched
skeleton walls and the roof, but the bridge didn't
shudder as the gusts struck it. If the water didn't
rise farther, the old bridge should be able to survive the flood.

He almost laughed at the thought. At the rate
the rain was coming down, even if it stopped that
very second, the water would continue to rise
for days. Sandbags wouldn't help. There was no
place to put them to divert the water away from

the bridge. Its future was in God's hands. There was nothing else Daniel could do to protect it.

Going to God should be your first choice, Daniel, not your last resort. His brother's voice echoed through his head as he glanced toward Hannah's house again.

Shock struck him anew. He'd known, of course, that the house was close to the creek, but now he noticed how it was on the same level above the water as the deck of the bridge. If the creek kept rising, her home was going to flood. The barn behind it should be fine, because it was set on higher ground.

Glancing once at the bridge, he prayed, *God, I'm leaving the bridge in Your hands, but please keep Hannah and her family safe in Your hands as well. Help me help them because I'm not sure I can do it alone.*

He ran to his buggy, knowing he couldn't hesitate. Hannah needed to evacuate along with her great-grandmother and Shelby.

Taffy shivered with fear as Daniel reached him.

"Let's go," Daniel urged, stroking the horse's nose.

The horse shifted his weight, and Daniel tugged on the bearing rein. He kept talking to Taffy as they walked into the storm, unsure if the horse was comforted by his voice. Or if the horse could hear it. Between the wind and the pounding rain, Daniel could barely hear his own voice.

He froze as he led a reluctant Taffy toward the Lambrights' house. Had he heard someone call his name? It must have been his imagination.

Then he heard it again. "Daniel, is that you?"

Hannah!

Tugging Taffy after him, he rushed up the muddy driveway. He saw her standing on the porch, waving. He left the horse and crossed the yard, leaping onto the porch. "You need to get out of here."

"I know." Her bonnet was a black, soggy mass around her face. Strands of her hair fell and stuck to her cheek. She shoved them back. "The Joneses have already left. They stopped to ask us to go with them."

"Why didn't you?"

"I tried to get *Grossmammi* Ella to go, but…" Her shrug said it all. Her great-grandmother had been too stubborn to leave.

"Let's get her and Shelby and go."

"Take them and go. I can't leave!"

"Hannah, I know things aren't right with us, but—"

"Daniel, it's the bees." Her eyes were frantic. "The bees are going to drown."

"Drown?"

"*Ja.* If the hives fill with water, they'll drown."

"Then let's move them."

She threw open the door and motioned for him to follow her. As he did, he was praying God would be merciful and save all of them.

Hannah retrieved her beekeeper's clothing. When it'd begun to rain hard last night, she'd brought it upstairs. Just to be prepared if the worst happened. Now it was.

While Shelby danced around them, excited, Hannah gave Daniel several pieces of the protective clothing for his use. His hands were too big for her gloves, but he pulled them on as best as he could. Taking rubber bands, he wrapped them around the long ends and the sleeves of his coat. The rain would keep most of the bees in the hive, but a few might dare the storm to protect their hive when it was moved. She insisted he wear her hat and veil.

"No, Hannah, you need it," he argued.

"I've got the smoker. If they panic and come toward me, I'll use it. You won't have anything to protect you. I can't have you flinch when you're carrying the hive. If it tumbles over, it could kill the queen bee and destroy the whole hive."

"But—"

"They most likely won't budge from the hive. I'll be fine." Not giving him time to reply, she turned to her great-grandmother who was sitting by the window and staring at the rising creek. "*Grossmammi* Ella," she said, making sure her voice remained calm, "we'll be in the backyard. Shelby has her toys, so she'll be fine until we get back."

"Be careful." The old woman's gaze went to Daniel. "Please be careful, Earney."

He didn't miss a beat as he said, "I will. Keep an eye on the creek and the covered bridge for me, won't you?"

"*Ja.*" Her great-grandmother straightened in her chair. "I will."

"*Danki.*" He tossed aside his straw hat. Pulling on the beekeeper's helmet, he didn't lower the veil over his face. "Let's get this over with."

When Hannah stepped outside, the rain seemed to be coming faster. She hadn't guessed that was possible. Her soaked bonnet clung to her hair like a deflated balloon.

She explained the easiest and safest way to move them was to lift the boards the hives sat on. They'd carry each hive into the barn as if it were on a litter.

When Daniel nodded he was ready and pulled down the veil, she smoked the closest of the three hives. The rain tore apart the smoke, so she wasn't sure how much reached the bees.

Keep them calm, she prayed as she set the smoker on the wet grass and bent to lift the hive.

It was heavier than she remembered, even with Daniel taking most of the weight on his side. They inched up the hill toward the barn. She saw bees gathering near the hive's entrance, but few ventured out. They were knocked to the ground by the rain, and she promised herself she'd try to find them once the hives were safe.

Setting the hive far enough inside the barn so it would stay dry, she hurried with Daniel to get the second one. When she asked him if he was all right, he nodded but said nothing.

They repeated the task twice, losing a few bees each time. Leaving Daniel to throw bright blue tarps over the hives to protect them further, she ran into the rain to collect the lost bees in her apron. They struggled as she set them on the floor near the hives. Each one must find its way to its own hive.

"Those are all I could find." She straightened and leaned against the low wall between the front of the barn and the stalls. Checking the tarps over the hives to make sure air could get to the bees, she listened to the hammering rain. Each drop sounded as if it were trying to pierce the roof.

The animals were restless, but she wasn't sure if the storm bothered them or the low hum of the bees. But they should be safe in the barn.

Wiping her wet hair from her eyes, she turned to Daniel who had taken off the beekeeper's helmet. He looked as soaked as she felt, but also incredibly handsome. His dark hair caught the faint light and glistened like his bright blue eyes. She wanted to stand there and drink in the sight of this man whom she'd loved almost from the moment they met.

She halted herself before she flung herself into his arms. Staring at the hives beneath the bright blue tarps, she said, "I couldn't have done it without you. *Danki.*"

"I'm glad to help." He undid the rubber bands and handed them and the gloves to her. "Once the storm is past, I'll help you move them back."

"You don't have to."

"You can't move them alone. I'll help…though I'd rather go to the dentist."

She laughed. "That's obvious. You should have seen your face. You looked like you were about to grab a poisonous snake."

"I'm leery of bees. That's no secret."

"And that's why I'm so grateful for your help. Not everyone would be able to get past their fears to touch the hives."

He put a hand on the wall behind her, standing closer than he had since they were in his house. He didn't touch her as he bent so their eyes were level. "With God's love, everything is possible. I believe that, and I've come to realize I need to live my belief every day." Each word brushed her damp face and touched her battered heart. "If I don't take the opportunities God makes available to me, I'm ignoring His blessings."

"You believe that? Really?" What a turnabout from his assumption he could handle everything on his own.

Lightning flashed and thunder crashed overhead, shaking the barn like a dog coming in from the rain.

"That was close." Daniel stepped away from her. "Let's go and get Shelby and your great-grandmother and get out of here."

She nodded. With one last check of the bees and the other animals, she ran with him out into the rain. She was drenched and cold by the time they reached the kitchen door.

"You get what you need for them," Daniel said, "while I help them put on their coats."

She nodded and hurried into the living room. It was empty.

"*Grossmammi* Ella! Shelby!" She ran to the bottom of the stairs, though her great-grandmother had not climbed them in a year. Had *Grossmammi* Ella decided to take Shelby up for her nap? The old woman wasn't steady enough to lift the toddler into her crib.

Taking the steps two at a time, she reached the top and called her great-grandmother's name and then her little sister's. Her voice echoed along the hallway. She pushed aside the nursery door, hoping *Grossmammi* Ella would be there and unharmed.

The room was as deserted as the first floor. Spinning, she ran down the stairs and collided with Daniel.

"Their coats are gone," he told her, his face pale.

"So are they! Where could they have gone in this storm?"

Chapter Sixteen

Hannah struggled to breathe. Had her great-grandmother wandered away, lost again in the past? She'd called Daniel by her late husband's name. Had she gone to find Earney? But why had her great-grandmother taken Shelby with her? That had never happened before.

"Oh, no!" groaned Daniel.

She whirled to look at him. "What?"

"I told *Grossmammi* Ella to watch the rising water and the bridge. Do you think she thought I meant she should watch the creek *from* the bridge?"

Horror sank through her. She scanned the room again as if she could find her great-grandmother on a second look. "I don't know what she'll do anymore."

"Hannah." His voice was so heavy she looked

at him and discovered his face had turned gray. "I never would have said that if I'd guessed—"

"I know you didn't. But we don't have time to discuss this. We need to find them!"

"C'mon!" He grabbed his hat and took her hand.

She raced with him from the house to where his horse stood in the unrelenting storm. The creek roared like a wounded beast was clawing its way onto the banks. The water level rose as she watched, pools gathering and combining on the road and along the creek. The new boards beneath the bridge were less than three inches above the rushing water.

When he turned toward the bridge, she grasped his sleeve. He didn't slow and almost jerked her off her feet.

"No!" she shouted over the din from the rushing water.

When he spoke, she had to guess what he was saying because his words were swallowed by the cacophony from the creek. He was asking why she was slowing him down. Or that's what she thought he'd said.

She tugged him toward the buggy. He looked at her as if she'd lost her mind. Standing on tiptoe, she knocked aside his hat so she could say into his ear, "We need to get the buggy."

He pointed at the covered bridge.

Hannah shook her head. Pulling on his arm again, she sent up a prayer of gratitude when he came with her. She threw open the buggy door and climbed in. Daniel did the same on the other side. The two doors shut at the same time, rocking the buggy, but the sound was lost beneath the rain striking the roof.

When he turned to her, she grimaced as rain sprayed off his hat's brim. She shook it off her face as she said, "*Grossmammi* Ella wouldn't have gone to the bridge. She hasn't gone to the bridge since the day you showed me where the bees are. She hates bees."

"Then where do you think they've gone?" Abrupt understanding burst into his eyes, followed an instant later by fear. "You think she took Shelby out to the old mill, ain't so?" He grasped the reins and slapped them on his horse to send the buggy along the flooded road.

Hannah clenched her hands. If she was wrong, they could be marooned out near the mill, and nobody else knew her great-grandmother and the toddler were missing.

Lord, guide us to them in time. The prayer resonated through her mind over and over in tempo with the horse's hooves.

Watching the road, Hannah leaned forward as if she could make the buggy move faster. Daniel guided Taffy around the biggest puddles, not wanting to mire the wheels, but each detour, no matter how small, seemed to lengthen the journey by miles instead of inches.

A hand settled over hers on the seat, and she tore her gaze from the road. Looking down, she saw Daniel's broad, workworn fingers atop hers. He squeezed her hand. The motion said more than words could have about how he shared her trepidation.

Tears welled in her eyes. If someone had told her yesterday that Daniel Stoltzfus would gauge her feelings accurately and care so much, she would have laughed with derision. What he'd said yesterday was true. The young, callous man he'd been, a man focused only on his dreams and ambitions…that man was gone. He'd been replaced by the Daniel sitting beside her, a warmhearted man who had told her that he'd changed.

And, though she'd tried to deny the truth, he *had* changed.

A lot.

As she had, because she wasn't the uncertain, desperate girl she'd been, wondering if anyone would love her after her *daed* abandoned her. She'd wondered if her great-grandmother saw her as anything other than an unwanted obligation dropped on her in her later years. How wrong she'd been! Discounting *Grossmammi* Ella's love as nothing but a duty had been her first mistake.

Believing she was unlovable was her second. Her *daed* had loved her, Shelby loved her, and...

Raising her eyes, she traced Daniel's profile. Was it possible he loved her, too? She loved him. She knew that as surely as she knew rain was falling.

Hannah rocked forward when the buggy came to a sudden stop. The road ahead was beneath water.

"We'll have to walk the rest of the way." Daniel threw open his door.

She jumped out and winced when the rain battered her. The wind tried to rock her off her feet as lightning flashed and thunder exploded around them. She was grateful when Daniel seized her hand and led her onto the side of the road so they could keep going.

As the old mill came into sight, it looked nothing as it had the last time she'd come out there. The crumbling walls were surrounded by water. The dam on the mill pond must be holding, though she wondered how long it could stand against the raging current.

She glanced toward it and pressed her hand to her mouth to silence her cry of alarm.

Her great-grandmother and Shelby stood hand-in-hand on top of the rickety dam. Waves splashed over it, and the whole structure trembled with the onslaught against it. Seeing Daniel looking in the other direction, she groaned. Farther up the creek, a tree slanted toward the water that had carved the earth away from its roots. If it toppled in, it would race like an arrow at the unstable dam.

Hannah ran as close as she could to the dam. She stood in ankle-high water, bracing herself to keep from being pulled in. Cupping her hands over her mouth, she shouted, "Shelby, come and see. Daniel's here."

The little girl's mouth moved, but the crash of the water stole the sound. She clutched her stuffed honeybee to her chest. Hannah wasn't sure if tears or the rain coursed down her round face.

"*Grossmammi* Ella, send Shelby to us. Please!"

For a moment, her great-grandmother's eyes focused on her and Daniel. Her gnarled fingers loosened on the toddler's hand.

Shelby teetered on the dam. When the little girl tumbled off her feet, Hannah's heart jumped into her throat. Somehow, the *kind* landed in the center of the top of the dam and held on to Buzz-buzz.

Hannah felt Daniel tense, but he kept her from moving forward as Shelby began crawling toward them.

"Don't spook your great-grandmother," he said close to her ear.

The moment Shelby reached the edge of the dam, Hannah held out her hands to the toddler. The little girl threw herself into Hannah's arms.

"Han-han!" she cried.

Hannah pressed her face against the *kind*'s soaked hair. Lifting her into her arms, she wept as the little girl wrapped her arms around her neck and clung to her. She moved backward, Daniel's hand gripping her arm to keep her feet from sliding out from under her on the slick slope.

"Get Shelby to the buggy," he said. "I'll get your great-grandmother."

"I need to—"

"You need to let me do this."

She shook her head, but didn't answer as a crack came from farther up the creek. The tree slipped closer to the water.

He took her by the shoulders. "Don't argue, Hannah. You've let others depend on you, but you've never been willing to depend on others. Why? Do you think it makes you powerless if you allow someone else to help you?"

"No, it's not that."

"Then what is it?"

She didn't have an answer for him, because having him come into her life again had led her to question how she lived her life as well as her expectations of herself and others.

"Hannah." He framed her face with his hands, tilting it so she could look into his eyes without having rain splash along her face. "You, of all people, should know how important it is for everyone to depend on each other. Your bees rely on each other to build their hive. If one fails, they all fail. That kind of dependence isn't weakness—it's strength."

He was right, but could she trust *Grossmammi* Ella's life to him? The answer came quickly. *Ja!* Even when he'd broken her heart, he'd been trying to do what was best for her. He'd helped her move the hives even though he hated being near bees. He'd won her heart…twice. How could she *not* trust him?

More important, she knew she could depend on him. He wasn't running away, torn between his conflicting dreams for his future. Her heart, no longer willing to be silent, called out she must give him another chance.

This chance.

She must depend on him to do what she couldn't: save her great-grandmother's life.

Shifting Shelby in her arms, she stepped toward the buggy. "Do what you can, Daniel, to save my great-grandmother."

Daniel was staggered by the strength of Hannah's belief in him. It shone from her eyes and flowed from her fingers as she clasped his arm. *Dear God, be with me so I don't disappoint Hannah again. Help me find the right words and do the right things to reach* Grossmammi *Ella.*

A sense of peace draped over him like an umbrella. Only this umbrella quieted a storm that had raged within him so long he'd learned to ignore it. In its wake seeped the warmth of knowing he wasn't alone. What had he told Hannah in the barn? With God's love, everything was possible. It was time for him to take his own words to heart.

He pulled his gaze from her great-grandmother. "Take Shelby and get in the buggy. Be ready to flee if the dam goes."

"Be careful." Her voice sounded like a whisper, but he guessed she was shouting as he was.

He nodded as Hannah hurried to the buggy. He didn't wait to see if she got in. No time for anything but getting her great-grandmother to safety.

His heart stopped in midbeat when he saw the tree topple into the creek, caught in an eddy. Once it escaped, it was going to hit the dam.

"*Grossmammi* Ella!" he called.

She ignored him.

He had to think of a way to reach her. He could run out and force her off, but he wasn't sure the dam could hold two adults. And there wasn't time to argue as she did except when she thought he was her late husband.

That was the answer!

"Ella!" he shouted. "Ella, *liebling*!"

The old woman's head snapped around like a marionette's. She stared at him and said something. Her words were lost in the noise, but he saw her lips form her husband's name.

"Ja!" He yelled louder. "Ella, *liebling*, come here to me. I know how much you miss your Earney." He chose his words carefully. He didn't want to lie to her.

"I've been waiting for you right here." She moved toward him. Slowly. Too slowly. "Right here where we used to watch the stars when we were courting."

He understood at last why she'd kept coming here. He'd share that with Hannah...later. For now, he had to chance going out to the old woman. As he put his foot on the dam, it seemed to sway beneath him. *Lord, I put our lives in Your hands.*

Running, he reached *Grossmammi* Ella. The dam was shaking with the current. He glanced to his right. The tree was on a collision course with the dam.

"Earney! I knew you'd come. I knew it!" The desperate cry came from deep within the old woman's heart as she collapsed in his arms.

He scooped her up and pulled his open coat around her to protect her from the storm. She couldn't weigh a hundred pounds. Shifting her so he didn't put pressure on her ancient bones, he turned to get off the dam.

He gasped when the windblown rain blinded him. He blinked, trying to see. When a hand grasped his elbow, pulling him to his left, he followed Hannah onto solid ground. He kept blinking hard, and his eyes cleared in time to see the buggy right in front of him.

He put *Grossmammi* Ella in next to Shelby who was watching with her thumb in her mouth, a sure sign the little girl was afraid. Motioning to Hannah to get in, he ran around to the other side. He jumped in and grabbed the reins, slapping them on the horse as soon as Hannah was inside.

Later, there would be time to thank her for guiding him to the buggy. Later, after they were safe. He shouted to the horse to go at its top speed.

Taffy must have understood the danger because the horse ran along the road, splashing water into the buggy through the open doors. He yanked his door closed and, from the corner of his eye, saw Hannah do the same on the other side.

"We've got to get up the hill," said *Gross-mammi* Ella in a matter-of-fact tone.

He knew that, but a fence edged the road. They could climb over, but he didn't want to leave Taffy behind.

"Over there!" Hannah pointed to an open gate barely visible in the rain.

"Take the reins! I'll help Taffy." He was out of the buggy before she could answer. As he slammed the door shut, he saw her grope for the reins.

Fighting his way through the fast-moving water, he grasped the horse's bridle. "Let's go, Taffy."

The water rose higher and higher as he led the horse toward the open gate. He watched, appalled, when the buggy slid sideways. He gritted his teeth and tried to move faster.

As soon as they reached the gate, Daniel slapped Taffy's rear to send the horse racing up the hill. He ran alongside and jumped in when Hannah threw the door open. He took the reins from her, fighting to keep the buggy upright as they bounced over the uneven ground.

At the top, he drew in the horse. Silence filled the buggy for the length of a single heartbeat.

He didn't hear the crash when the tree struck, but the dam collapsing was as loud as the thunder overhead. Shrieks came from the toddler and

Grossmammi Ella. Hannah hushed them before she scrambled out of the buggy.

Daniel jumped out and came around to where she stood. He grasped her shoulders and spun her so her back was to the scene of destruction below them.

"Look at Taffy." He clasped her face between his hands to keep her from seeing the maddened creek. "Or better yet, look at me, Hannah. Look at me, and don't look away."

"I don't want to look anywhere else."

"*Gut!* Look at me, and I'll look at you. Nowhere else."

Crashes came from below, and she shuddered. "Don't you want to see what's happening to the bridge?"

He shook his head. "We fixed it once. We can fix it again."

"*Danki* for saving us." She rested her head against his chest, and he knew she must be able to hear his heart thud with the joy of holding her close.

"*Danki* for trusting me." He leaned his cheek against the top of her ruined bonnet.

"I always will." She raised her gaze to his. "Always."

"And I'll never give you a reason to believe you can't depend on me again."

She tightened her hold around him as he

claimed her lips. As crashes heralded damage along the creek, he held her close as he found everything he wanted in her kiss.

Chapter Seventeen

"Excellent work, Daniel." Liam O'Neill's booming voice echoed in the covered bridge like the metal buggy wheels of an Amish buggy on the deck. "I didn't know if this old bridge would still be standing, but it seems you saved it."

"The *gut* Lord did," Daniel replied, giving credit where it was due.

"By giving you and your crew the skills to strengthen it in time for the flood." The Irishman glanced at the tools and scrap wood piled on the deck. The debris had been swept out yesterday. "When will you be done here?"

"It's going to take us another few weeks. The flood did enough damage that we have to check each bridge support and replace the missing ones as well as those that were weakened." He glanced along the bridge and tried to quell the pulse of pride that nearly all the repairs had survived the flood.

The repairs hadn't been just his work. They'd been his and his crew's work. It'd taken him long enough to see one man couldn't do the work alone. A leader's job was to find the best men for the job and let them do it.

More than a week had passed before the waters retreated enough for him to assess the full damage. The waterline inside the bridge was almost two feet above the deck, but the reinforced bridge had stood. The days had been fair and warm, a gift from God in the wake of the month of rain and floods. During that time, Liam had offered him the project he wanted Stoltzfus Brothers Construction to oversee.

Stoltzfus Brothers Construction. The name seemed perfect, because he intended to use his brothers' skills whenever a job required them. Primarily his twin, since he'd asked Micah if he'd like to become his partner in the business. Micah told him he needed time to consider the offer, surprising Daniel. That sounded like their cautious brother Jeremiah instead of his twin who usually looked while he was leaping.

"After you've checked out the bridge, you plan to start on my project?" asked Liam.

"*Ja.*"

"Excellent." He glanced past Daniel. "You've got some people waiting to talk to you."

Looking over his shoulder, Daniel smiled when he saw Hannah standing on the other side of the concrete barrier. Shelby clung to her as the *kind* had since they fled the flood. He hoped the toddler would soon forget the experience, though he knew he never would. Every night since that harrowing escape, he'd had nightmares about the waters overtaking them after he'd asked Hannah to depend on him—truly depend on him for the first time.

Thanking Liam, Daniel walked over to where Hannah stood by their buggy. "Where's *Gross-mammi* Ella?"

"At the time we left your family's house, she was trying to teach your *mamm* to make *snitz* pie."

"My *mamm* makes the best *snitz* pie in the county." He grinned. "Maybe the whole world."

"You know that. I know that. Wanda knows that, though she'd never be so prideful as to admit it. But my great-grandmother doesn't know that, and she's sure Wanda can learn a lot from her."

"We all can."

"And we'll have the time to do that, thanks to you saving her."

He tapped her nose as if she were no older than

Shelby. "Don't you remember what I've said so often? Let's leave the past in the past?"

"I agree. I'd rather look to the future, too." She glanced at her home which was leaning from where the strong current had pushed it off its foundation. A tree trunk had impaled itself in the center of the porch, and branches and other debris tumbled out the front door.

But the three hives had escaped the flood in the barn along with the other animals. The chickens hadn't left their roosts under the roof. Judging by their hoofprints, the two cows had gone no farther than the field beyond the barn. Both had returned by the time Hannah was able to check on them.

"Do you want to look in the windows?" he asked.

"I already did. There's nothing left inside worth saving. Everything either washed away or is ruined beyond repair." She set Shelby on the buggy seat and smiled as her little sister cuddled her stuffed bumblebee. "I'm so grateful Shelby had Buzz-buzz with her when *Grossmammi* Ella took her to the mill."

"*Grossmammi* Ella saved our lives." He rested his elbow on the side of the door. "If your great-grandmother hadn't rushed off so we had to give chase, we could have been in the house and never known what was coming at us until it was too late to escape."

"I've thanked her, but I don't think she understands why. And I've thanked God for keeping us safe."

"As I have." He slipped his arm around her waist. "You know, I've been thinking."

"Uh-oh, that could mean trouble."

He chuckled. "Usually, but this time you'll like what I'm thinking. The house is cramped with your family living with mine, so you and Shelby and your great-grandmother should move to my house."

"Didn't you build it for your brother and his future wife?"

"That wife is further in the future every day because he can't get up the nerve to talk to her." He curved his hand along her face. "Hannah, I built the house for a family. So why don't you move in? I'll join you after we get married."

"Married?" she gasped.

"Isn't that what people in love do? Get married?" He leaned into the buggy. "I love you, Hannah Lambright. I always have. I was too young and foolish and proud to admit it three years ago."

"But your business—"

"Will always be secondary to my wife and our family. I believed owning a business was my dream, but I never realized the best reason for having my own company was being able to provide a *gut* home for the ones I love. You and Shelby and *Grossmammi* Ella. We'll take care of each other and watch over each other. Will you marry me, Hannah?"

"*Ja*, because I love you, too, Daniel," she whispered as she stood on tiptoe and pressed her lips to his.

He swept his arms around her and kissed her, knowing *all* his dreams were finally coming true.

* * * * *

Don't miss these other AMISH HEARTS *stories from Jo Ann Brown:*

AMISH HOMECOMING
AN AMISH MATCH
HIS AMISH SWEETHEART

Find more great reads at
www.LoveInspired.com.

Dear Reader,

It's easy to get caught up in obligations and forget that there are others who are willing to help us. For those with a volunteer's heart, the ones who always are there to help, it's sometimes difficult to accept assistance from others. Learning that it's important to let others relish the joy of helping you can be a hard lesson. I know it was for Hannah…and for me. But once I discovered that givers must learn to receive as well, I found my friendships were deepened and I got more satisfaction from helping because I came to understand what it meant to be helped. Both Hannah and Daniel do as well, and their lives are enriched with love.

Stop in and visit me at www.joann brownbooks.com. Look for my next story in the Amish Hearts series coming soon.

Wishing you many blessings,
Jo Ann Brown

REQUEST YOUR FREE BOOKS!
2 FREE RIVETING INSPIRATIONAL NOVELS
PLUS 2 FREE MYSTERY GIFTS

Love Inspired®
SUSPENSE
RIVETING INSPIRATIONAL ROMANCE

YES! Please send me 2 FREE Love Inspired® Suspense novels and my 2 FREE mystery gifts (gifts are worth about $10). After receiving them, if I don't wish to receive any more books, I can return the shipping statement marked "cancel." If I don't cancel, I will receive 4 brand-new novels every month and be billed just $4.99 per book in the U.S. or $5.49 per book in Canada. That's a savings of at least 17% off the cover price. It's quite a bargain! Shipping and handling is just 50¢ per book in the U.S. and 75¢ per book in Canada.* I understand that accepting the 2 free books and gifts places me under no obligation to buy anything. I can always return a shipment and cancel at any time. Even if I never buy another book, the two free books and gifts are mine to keep forever.

123/323 IDN GH5Z

Name	(PLEASE PRINT)	

Address		Apt. #

City	State/Prov.	Zip/Postal Code

Signature (if under 18, a parent or guardian must sign)

Mail to the **Reader Service:**
IN U.S.A.: P.O. Box 1867, Buffalo, NY 14240-1867
IN CANADA: P.O. Box 609, Fort Erie, Ontario L2A 5X3

**Are you a current subscriber to Love Inspired® Suspense books
and want to receive the larger-print edition?
Call 1-800-873-8635 or visit www.ReaderService.com.**

* Terms and prices subject to change without notice. Prices do not include applicable taxes. Sales tax applicable in N.Y. Canadian residents will be charged applicable taxes. Offer not valid in Quebec. This offer is limited to one order per household. Not valid for current subscribers to Love Inspired Suspense books. All orders subject to credit approval. Credit or debit balances in a customer's account(s) may be offset by any other outstanding balance owed by or to the customer. Please allow 4 to 6 weeks for delivery. Offer available while quantities last.

Your Privacy—The Reader Service is committed to protecting your privacy. Our Privacy Policy is available online at www.ReaderService.com or upon request from the Reader Service.
We make a portion of our mailing list available to reputable third parties that offer products we believe may interest you. If you prefer that we not exchange your name with third parties, or if you wish to clarify or modify your communication preferences, please visit us at www.ReaderService.com/consumerchoice or write to us at Reader Service Preference Service, P.O. Box 9062, Buffalo, NY 14240-9062. Include your complete name and address.

LIS15

REQUEST YOUR FREE BOOKS!
2 FREE WHOLESOME ROMANCE NOVELS IN LARGER PRINT
PLUS 2
FREE
MYSTERY GIFTS

✻ ✻

HEARTWARMING™

❦ ❦

Wholesome, tender romances

YES! Please send me 2 FREE Harlequin® Heartwarming Larger-Print novels and my 2 FREE mystery gifts (gifts worth about \$10). After receiving them, if I don't wish to receive any more books, I can return the shipping statement marked "cancel." If I don't cancel, I will receive 4 brand-new larger-print novels every month and be billed just \$5.24 per book in the U.S. or \$5.99 per book in Canada. That's a savings of at least 19% off the cover price. It's quite a bargain! Shipping and handling is just 50¢ per book in the U.S. and 75¢ per book in Canada.* I understand that accepting the 2 free books and gifts places me under no obligation to buy anything. I can always return a shipment and cancel at any time. Even if I never buy another book, the two free books and gifts are mine to keep forever.

161/361 IDN GHX2

Name   (PLEASE PRINT)

Address   Apt. #

City   State/Prov.   Zip/Postal Code

Signature (if under 18, a parent or guardian must sign)

Mail to the **Reader Service:**
IN U.S.A.: P.O. Box 1867, Buffalo, NY 14240-1867
IN CANADA: P.O. Box 609, Fort Erie, Ontario L2A 5X3

* Terms and prices subject to change without notice. Prices do not include applicable taxes. Sales tax applicable in N.Y. Canadian residents will be charged applicable taxes. Offer not valid in Quebec. This offer is limited to one order per household. Not valid for current subscribers to Harlequin Heartwarming larger-print books. All orders subject to credit approval. Credit or debit balances in a customer's account(s) may be offset by any other outstanding balance owed by or to the customer. Please allow 4 to 6 weeks for delivery. Offer available while quantities last.

Your Privacy—The Reader Service is committed to protecting your privacy. Our Privacy Policy is available online at www.ReaderService.com or upon request from the Reader Service.

We make a portion of our mailing list available to reputable third parties that offer products we believe may interest you. If you prefer that we not exchange your name with third parties, or if you wish to clarify or modify your communication preferences, please visit us at www.ReaderService.com/consumerschoice or write to us at Reader Service Preference Service, P.O. Box 9062, Buffalo, NY 14240-9062. Include your complete name and address.

HW15

WESTERN WP PROMISES

YES! Please send me **The Western Promises Collection** in Larger Print. This collection begins with 3 FREE books and 2 FREE gifts (gifts valued at approx. $14.00 retail) in the first shipment, along with the other first 4 books from the collection! If I do not cancel, I will receive 8 monthly shipments until I have the entire 51-book Western Promises collection. I will receive 2 or 3 FREE books in each shipment and I will pay just $4.99 US/ $5.89 CDN for each of the other four books in each shipment, plus $2.99 for shipping and handling per shipment. *If I decide to keep the entire collection, I'll have paid for only 32 books, because 19 books are FREE! I understand that accepting the 3 free books and gifts places me under no obligation to buy anything. I can always return a shipment and cancel at any time. My free books and gifts are mine to keep no matter what I decide.

272 HCN 3070 472 HCN 3070

Name	(PLEASE PRINT)	
Address		Apt. #
City	State/Prov.	Zip/Postal Code

Signature (if under 18, a parent or guardian must sign)

Mail to the **Reader Service:**
IN U.S.A.: P.O. Box 1867, Buffalo, NY 14240-1867
IN CANADA: P.O. Box 609, Fort Erie, Ontario L2A 5X3

* Terms and prices subject to change without notice. Prices do not include applicable taxes. Sales tax applicable in N.Y. Canadian residents will be charged applicable taxes. This offer is limited to one order per household. All orders subject to approval. Credit or debit balances in a customer's account(s) may be offset by any other outstanding balance owed by or to the customer. Please allow 4 to 6 weeks for delivery. Offer available while quantities last. Offer not available to Quebec residents.

(I) READERSERVICE.COM

Manage your account online!

- Review your order history
- Manage your payments
- Update your address

> ### *We've designed the Reader Service website just for you.*

Enjoy all the features!

- Discover new series available to you, and read excerpts from any series.
- Respond to mailings and special monthly offers.
- Connect with favorite authors at the blog.
- Browse the Bonus Bucks catalog and online-only exculsives.
- Share your feedback.

Visit us at:

ReaderService.com

RS15